# The Battle of the Books
## and Other Short Pieces

*Jonathan Swift*

# Contents

# THE BATTLE OF THE BOOKS
# AND OTHER SHORT PIECES

BY

Jonathan Swift

# INTRODUCTION.

Jonathan Swift was born in 1667, on the 30th of November. His father was a Jonathan Swift, sixth of the ten sons of the Rev. Thomas Swift, vicar of Goodrich, near Ross, in Herefordshire, who had married Elizabeth Dryden, niece to the poet Dryden's grandfather. Jonathan Swift married, at Leicester, Abigail Erick, or Herrick, who was of the family that had given to England Robert Herrick, the poet. As their eldest brother, Godwin, was prospering in Ireland, four other Swifts, Dryden, William, Jonathan, and Adam, all in turn found their way to Dublin. Jonathan was admitted an attorney of the King's Inns, Dublin, and was appointed by the Benchers to the office of Steward of the King's Inns, in January, 1666. He died in April, 1667, leaving his widow with an infant daughter, Jane, and an unborn child.

Swift was born in Dublin seven months after his father's death. His mother after a time returned to her own family, in Leicester, and the child was added to the household of his uncle, Godwin Swift, who, by his four wives, became father to ten sons of his own and four daughters. Godwin Swift sent his nephew to Kilkenny School, where he had William Congreve among his schoolfellows. In April, 1782, Swift was entered at Trinity College as pensioner, together with his cousin Thomas, son of his uncle Thomas. That cousin Thomas afterwards became rector of Puttenham, in Surrey. Jonathan Swift graduated as B.A. at Dublin, in February, 1686, and remained in Trinity College for another three years. He was ready to proceed to M.A. when his uncle Godwin became insane. The troubles of 1689 also caused the closing of the University, and Jonathan Swift went to Leicester, where mother and son took counsel together as to future possibilities of life.

The retired statesman, Sir William Temple, at Moor Park, near Farnham, in

Surrey, was in highest esteem with the new King and the leaders of the Revolution. His father, as Master of the Irish Rolls, had been a friend of Godwin Swift's, and with his wife Swift's mother could claim cousinship. After some months, therefore, at Leicester, Jonathan Swift, aged twenty-two, went to Moor Park, and entered Sir William Temple's household, doing service with the expectation of advancement through his influence. The advancement he desired was in the Church. When Swift went to Moor Park he found in its household a child six or seven years old, daughter to Mrs. Johnson, who was trusted servant and companion to Lady Gifford, Sir William Temple's sister. With this little Esther, aged seven, Swift, aged twenty-two, became a playfellow and helper in her studies. He broke his English for her into what he called their "little language," that was part of the same playful kindliness, and passed into their after-life. In July, 1692, with Sir William Temple's help, Jonathan Swift commenced M.A. in Oxford, as of Hart Hall. In 1694, Swift's ambition having been thwarted by an offer of a clerkship, of 120 pounds a year, in the Irish Rolls, he broke from Sir William Temple, took orders, and obtained, through other influence, in January, 1695, the small prebendary of Kilroot, in the north of Ireland. He was there for about a year. Close by, in Belfast, was an old college friend, named Waring, who had a sister. Swift was captivated by Miss Waring, called her Varina, and would have become engaged to marry her if she had not flinched from engagement with a young clergyman whose income was but a hundred a year.

But Sir William Temple had missed Jonathan Swift from Moor Park. Differences were forgotten, and Swift, at his wish, went back. This was in 1696, when his little pupil, Esther Johnson, was fifteen. Swift said of her, "I knew her from six years old, and had some share in her education, by directing what books she should read, and perpetually instructing her in the principles of honour and virtue, from which she never swerved in any one action or moment of her life. She was sickly from her childhood until about the age of fifteen; but then grew into perfect health, and was then looked upon as one of the most beautiful, graceful, and agreeable young women in London, only a little too fat. Her hair was blacker than a raven, and every feature of her face in perfection." This was the Stella of Swift's after-life, the one woman to whom his whole love was given. But side by side with the slow growth of his knowledge of all she was for him, was the slow growth of his conviction that attacks of giddiness and deafness, which first came when he was twenty, and recurred at times throughout his life, were signs to be associated with that which he regarded as the curse upon his life. His end would be like his uncle Godwin's. It was a curse transmissible to children, but if he desired to keep the influence his genius gave him, he could not tell the world why he refused to marry. Only to Stella, who remained unmarried for his sake, and gave her life to him, could all be known.

Returned to Moor Park, Swift wrote, in 1697, the "Battle of the Books," as well as the "Tale of the Tub," with which it was published seven years afterwards, in 1704. Perrault and others had been battling in France over the relative merits of Ancient and Modern Writers. The debate had spread to England. On behalf of the Ancients, stress was laid by Temple on the letters of Phalaris, tyrant of Agrigentum. Wotton replied to Sir William for the Moderns. The Hon. Charles Boyle, of Christ Church, published a new edition of the Epistles of Phalaris, with translation of the Greek text into Latin. Dr. Bentley, the King's Librarian, published a "Dissertation on the Epistles of Phalaris," denying their value, and arguing that Phalaris did not write them. Christ Church replied through Charles Boyle, with "Dr. Bentley's Dissertation on the Epistles of Phalaris examined." Swift entered into the war with a light heart, and matched the Ancients in defending them for the amusement of his patron. His incidental argument between the Spider and the Bee has provided a catch-phrase, "Sweetness and Light," to a combatant of later times.

Sir William Temple died on the 27th of January, 1699. Swift then became chaplain to Lord Berkeley in Dublin Castle, and it was as a little surprise to Lady Berkeley, who liked him to read to her Robert Boyle's "Meditations," that Swift wrote the "Meditation on a Broomstick." In February, 1700, he obtained from Lord Berkeley the vicarage of Laracor with the living of Rathbeggan, also in the diocese of Meath. In the beginning of 1701 Esther Johnson, to whom Sir William Temple had bequeathed a leasehold farm in Wicklow, came with an elder friend, Miss Dingley, and settled in Laracor to be near Swift. During one of the visits to London, made from Laracor, Swift attacked the false pretensions of astrologers by that prediction of the death of Mr. Partridge, a prophetic almanac maker, of which he described the Accomplishment so clearly that Partridge had much ado to get credit for being alive.

The lines addressed to Stella speak for themselves. "Cadenus and Vanessa" was meant as polite and courteous admonition to Miss Hester Van Homrigh, a young lady in whom green-sickness seems to have produced devotion to Swift in forms that embarrassed him, and with which he did not well know how to deal.

H. M.

# THE BOOKSELLER TO THE READER.

This discourse, as it is unquestionably of the same author, so it seems to have been written about the same time, with "The Tale of a Tub;" I mean the year 1697, when the famous dispute was on foot about ancient and modern learning. The controversy took its rise from an essay of Sir William Temple's upon that subject; which was answered by W. Wotton, B.D., with an appendix by Dr. Bentley, endeavouring to destroy the credit of AEsop and Phalaris for authors, whom Sir William Temple had, in the essay before mentioned, highly commended. In that appendix the doctor falls hard upon a new edition of Phalaris, put out by the Honourable Charles Boyle, now Earl of Orrery, to which Mr. Boyle replied at large with great learning and wit; and the Doctor voluminously rejoined. In this dispute the town highly resented to see a person of Sir William Temple's character and merits roughly used by the two reverend gentlemen aforesaid, and without any manner of provocation. At length, there appearing no end of the quarrel, our author tells us that the BOOKS in St. James's Library, looking upon themselves as parties principally concerned, took up the controversy, and came to a decisive battle; but the manuscript, by the injury of fortune or weather, being in several places imperfect, we cannot learn to which side the victory fell.

I must warn the reader to beware of applying to persons what is here meant only of books, in the most literal sense. So, when Virgil is mentioned, we are not to understand the person of a famous poet called by that name; but only certain sheets of paper bound up in leather, containing in print the works of the said poet: and so of the rest.

# THE PREFACE OF THE AUTHOR.

Satire is a sort of glass wherein beholders do generally discover everybody's face but their own; which is the chief reason for that kind reception it meets with in the world, and that so very few are offended with it. But, if it should happen otherwise, the danger is not great; and I have learned from long experience never to apprehend mischief from those understandings I have been able to provoke: for anger and fury, though they add strength to the sinews of the body, yet are found to relax those of the mind, and to render all its efforts feeble and impotent.

There is a brain that will endure but one scumming; let the owner gather it with discretion, and manage his little stock with husbandry; but, of all things, let him beware of bringing it under the lash of his betters, because that will make it all bubble up into impertinence, and he will find no new supply. Wit without knowledge being a sort of cream, which gathers in a night to the top, and by a skilful hand may be soon whipped into froth; but once scummed away, what appears underneath will be fit for nothing but to be thrown to the hogs.

A FULL AND TRUE ACCOUNT OF THE BATTLE FOUGHT LAST FRIDAY BETWEEN THE ANCIENT AND THE MODERN BOOKS IN SAINT JAMES'S LIBRARY.

Whoever examines, with due circumspection, into the annual records of time, will find it remarked that War is the child of Pride, and Pride the daughter of Riches:--the former of which assertions may be soon granted, but one cannot so easily subscribe to the latter; for Pride is nearly related to Beggary and Want, either by father or mother, and sometimes by both: and, to speak naturally, it very seldom happens among men to fall out when all have enough; invasions usually travelling from north to south, that is to say, from poverty to plenty. The most ancient and natural grounds of quarrels are lust and avarice; which, though we may allow to be brethren, or collateral branches of pride, are certainly the issues of want. For, to speak in the phrase of writers upon politics, we may observe in the republic of dogs, which in its original seems to be an institution of the many, that the whole state is ever in the profoundest peace after a full meal; and that civil broils arise among them when it happens for one great bone to be seized on by some leading dog, who either divides it among the few, and then it falls to an oligarchy, or keeps it to himself, and then it runs up to a tyranny. The same reasoning also holds place among them in those dissensions we behold upon a turgescency in any of their females. For the right of possession lying in common (it being impossible to establish a property in so delicate a case), jealousies and suspicions do so abound, that the whole commonwealth of that street is reduced to a manifest state of war, of every citizen against every citizen, till some one of more courage, conduct, or fortune than the rest seizes and enjoys the prize: upon which naturally arises plenty of heart-burning, and envy, and snarling against the happy dog. Again, if we look upon any of these republics engaged in a foreign war, either of invasion or defence, we shall find the same reasoning will serve as to the grounds and occasions of each; and that poverty or want, in some degree or other (whether real or in opinion, which makes no alteration in the case), has a great share, as well as pride, on the part of the aggressor.

Now whoever will please to take this scheme, and either reduce or adapt it to an intellectual state or commonwealth of learning, will soon discover the first ground of disagreement between the two great parties at this time in arms, and may form just conclusions upon the merits of either cause. But the issue or events of this war are not so easy to conjecture at; for the present quarrel is so inflamed by the warm heads of either faction, and the pretensions somewhere or other so exorbitant, as not to admit the least overtures of accommodation. This quarrel first began, as I have heard it affirmed by an old dweller in the neighbourhood, about a small spot of ground, lying and being upon one of the two tops of the hill Parnassus; the highest and largest of which had, it seems, been time out of mind in quiet possession of certain tenants, called the Ancients; and the other was held by the Moderns. But these disliking their present station, sent certain ambassadors to the Ancients, complaining of a great nuisance; how the height of that part of Parnassus quite spoiled the prospect of theirs, especially towards the east; and therefore, to avoid a war, offered them the choice of this alternative, either that the Ancients would please to remove themselves and their effects down to the lower summit, which the Moderns would graciously surrender to them, and advance into their place; or else the said Ancients will give leave to the Moderns to come with shovels and mattocks, and level the said hill as low as they shall think it convenient. To which the Ancients made answer, how little they expected such a message as this from a colony whom they had admitted, out of their own free grace, to so near a neighbourhood. That, as to their own seat, they were aborigines of it, and therefore to talk with them of a removal or surrender was a language they did not understand. That if the height of the hill on their side shortened the prospect of the Moderns, it was a disadvantage they could not help; but desired them to consider whether that injury (if it be any) were not largely recompensed by the shade and shelter it afforded them. That as to the levelling or digging down, it was either folly or ignorance to propose it if they did or did not know how that side of the hill was an entire rock, which would break their tools and hearts, without any damage to itself. That they would therefore advise the Moderns rather to raise their own side of the hill than dream of pulling down that of the Ancients; to the former of which they would not only give licence, but also largely contribute. All this was rejected by the Moderns with much indignation, who still insisted upon one of the two expedients; and so this difference broke out into a long and obstinate war, maintained on the one part by resolution, and by the courage of certain leaders and allies; but, on the other, by the greatness of their number, upon all defeats affording continual recruits. In this quarrel whole rivulets of ink have been exhausted, and the virulence of both parties enormously augmented. Now, it must be here understood, that ink is the great missive weapon in all battles of the learned, which, conveyed through a sort of engine called a quill, infinite numbers of these are darted at the enemy by the valiant on each side, with equal skill and violence, as if it were an engagement of porcupines. This malignant liquor was compounded, by the engineer who invented it, of two ingredients, which are, gall and copperas; by its bitterness and venom to suit, in some degree, as well as to foment, the genius of the combatants. And as the Grecians, after an engagement, when they could not agree about the victory, were wont to set up trophies on both sides, the beaten party being content to be at the same expense, to keep itself in countenance (a laudable and ancient custom, happily revived of late in the art of war), so the learned, after a sharp and bloody dispute, do, on both sides, hang out their trophies too, whichever comes by the worst. These trophies have largely inscribed on them the merits of the cause; a full impartial account of such a Battle, and how the victory fell clearly to the party that set them up. They are known to the world under several names; as disputes, arguments, rejoinders, brief considerations, answers, replies, remarks, reflections, objections, confutations. For a very few days they are fixed up all in public places, either by themselves or their representatives, for passengers to gaze at; whence the chiefest and largest are removed to certain magazines they call libraries, there to remain in a quarter purposely assigned them, and thenceforth begin to be called books of controversy.

In these books is wonderfully instilled and preserved the spirit of each warrior while he is alive; and after his death his soul transmigrates thither to inform them. This, at least, is the more common opinion; but I believe it is with libraries as with other cemeteries, where some philosophers affirm that a certain spirit, which they call *brutum hominis*, hovers over the monument, till the body is corrupted and turns to dust or to worms, but then vanishes or dissolves; so, we may say, a restless spirit haunts over every book, till dust or worms have seized upon it--which to some may happen in a few days, but to others later--and therefore, books of controversy being, of all others, haunted by the most disorderly spirits, have always been confined in a separate lodge from the rest, and for fear of a mutual violence against each other, it was thought prudent by our ancestors to bind them to the peace with strong iron chains. Of which invention the original occasion was this: When the works of Scotus first came out, they were carried to a certain library, and had lodgings appointed them; but this author was no sooner settled than he went to visit his master Aristotle, and there both concerted together to seize Plato by main force, and turn him out from his ancient station among the divines, where he had peaceably dwelt near eight hundred years. The attempt succeeded, and the two usurpers have reigned ever since in his stead; but, to maintain quiet for the future, it was decreed that all polemics of the larger size should be hold fast with a chain.

By this expedient, the public peace of libraries might certainly have been preserved if a new species of controversial books had not arisen of late years, instinct with a more malignant spirit, from the war above mentioned between the learned about the higher summit of Parnassus.

When these books were first admitted into the public libraries, I remember to have said, upon occasion, to several persons concerned, how I was sure they would create broils wherever they came, unless a world of care were taken; and therefore I advised that the champions of each side should be coupled together, or otherwise mixed, that, like the blending of contrary poisons, their malignity might be employed among themselves. And it seems I was neither an ill prophet nor an ill counsellor; for it was nothing else but the neglect of this caution which gave occasion to the terrible fight that happened on Friday last between the Ancient and Modern Books in the King's library. Now, because the talk of this battle is so fresh in everybody's mouth, and the expectation of the town so great to be informed in the particulars, I, being possessed of all qualifications requisite in an historian, and retained by neither party, have resolved to comply with the urgent importunity of my friends, by writing down a full impartial account thereof.

The guardian of the regal library, a person of great valour, but chiefly renowned for his humanity, had been a fierce champion for the Moderns, and, in an engagement upon Parnassus, had vowed with his own hands to knock down two of the ancient chiefs who guarded a small pass on the superior rock, but, endeavouring to climb up, was cruelly obstructed by his own unhappy weight and tendency towards his centre, a quality to which those of the Modern party are extremely subject; for, being light- headed, they have, in speculation, a wonderful agility, and conceive nothing too high for them to mount, but, in reducing to practice, discover a mighty pressure about their posteriors and their heels. Having thus failed in his design, the disappointed champion bore a cruel rancour to the Ancients, which he resolved to gratify by showing all marks of his favour to the books of their adversaries, and lodging them in the fairest apartments; when, at the same time, whatever book had the boldness to own itself for an advocate of the Ancients was buried alive in some obscure corner, and threatened, upon the least displeasure, to be turned out of doors. Besides, it so happened that about this time there was a strange confusion of place among all the books in the library, for which several reasons were assigned. Some imputed it to a great heap of learned dust, which a perverse wind blew off from a shelf of Moderns into the keeper's eyes. Others affirmed he had a humour to pick the worms out of the schoolmen, and swallow them fresh and fasting, whereof some fell upon his spleen, and some climbed up into his head, to the great perturbation of both. And lastly, others maintained that, by walking much in the dark about the library, he had quite lost the situation of it out of his head; and therefore, in replacing his books, he was apt to mistake and clap Descartes next to Aristotle, poor Plato had got between Hobbes and the Seven Wise Masters, and Virgil was hemmed in with Dryden on one side and Wither on the other.

Meanwhile, those books that were advocates for the Moderns, chose out one from among them to make a progress through the whole library, examine the number and strength of their party, and concert their affairs. This messenger performed all things very industriously, and brought back with him a list of their forces, in all, fifty thousand, consisting chiefly of light-horse, heavy-armed foot, and mercenaries; whereof the foot were in general but sorrily armed and worse clad; their horses large, but extremely out of case and heart; however, some few, by trading among the Ancients, had furnished themselves tolerably enough.

While things were in this ferment, discord grew extremely high; hot words passed on both sides, and ill blood was plentifully bred. Here a solitary Ancient, squeezed up among a whole shelf of Moderns, offered fairly to dispute the case, and to prove by manifest reason that the priority was due to them from long possession, and in regard of their prudence, antiquity, and, above all, their great merits toward the Moderns. But these denied the premises, and seemed very much to wonder how the Ancients could pretend to insist upon their antiquity, when it was so plain (if they went to that) that the Moderns were much the more ancient of the two. As for any obligations they owed to the Ancients, they renounced them all. "It is true," said they, "we are informed some few of our party have been so mean as to borrow their subsistence from you, but the rest, infinitely the greater number (and especially we French and English), were so far from stooping to so base an example, that there never passed, till this very hour, six words between us. For our horses were of our own breeding, our arms of our own forging, and our clothes of our own cutting out and sewing." Plato was by chance up on the next shelf, and observing those that spoke to be in the ragged plight mentioned a while ago, their jades lean and foundered, their weapons of rotten wood, their armour rusty, and nothing but rags underneath, he laughed loud, and in his pleasant way swore, by ---, he believed them.

Now, the Moderns had not proceeded in their late negotiation with secrecy enough to escape the notice of the enemy. For those advocates who had begun the quarrel, by setting first on foot the dispute of precedency, talked so loud of coming to a battle, that Sir William Temple happened to overhear them, and gave immediate intelligence to the Ancients, who thereupon drew up their scattered troops together, resolving to act upon the defensive; upon which, several of the Moderns fled over to their party, and among the rest Temple himself. This Temple, having been educated and long conversed among the Ancients, was, of all the Moderns, their greatest favourite, and became their greatest champion.

Things were at this crisis when a material accident fell out. For upon the highest corner of a large window, there dwelt a certain spider, swollen up to the first magnitude by the destruction of infinite numbers of flies, whose spoils lay scattered before the gates of his palace, like human bones before the cave of some giant. The avenues to his castle were guarded with turnpikes and palisadoes, all after the modern way of fortification. After you had passed several courts you came to the centre, wherein you might behold the constable himself in his own lodgings, which had windows fronting to each avenue, and ports to sally out upon all occasions of prey or defence. In this mansion he had for some time dwelt in peace and plenty, without danger to his person by swallows from above, or to his palace by brooms from below; when it was the pleasure of fortune to conduct thither a wandering bee, to whose curiosity a broken pane in the glass had discovered itself, and in he went, where, expatiating a while, he at last happened to alight upon one of the outward walls of the spider's citadel; which, yielding to the unequal weight, sunk down to the very foundation. Thrice he endeavoured to force his passage, and thrice the centre shook. The spider within, feeling the terrible convulsion, supposed at first that nature was approaching to her final dissolution, or else that Beelzebub, with all his legions, was come to revenge the death of many thousands of his subjects whom his enemy had slain and devoured. However, he at length valiantly resolved to issue forth and meet his fate. Meanwhile the bee had acquitted himself of his toils, and, posted securely at some distance, was employed in cleansing his wings, and disengaging them from the ragged remnants of the cobweb. By this time the spider was adventured out, when, beholding the chasms, the ruins, and dilapidations of his fortress, he was very near at his wit's end; he stormed and swore like a madman, and swelled till he was ready to burst. At length, casting his eye upon the bee, and wisely gathering causes from events (for they know each other by sight), "A plague split you," said he; "is it you, with a vengeance, that have made this litter here; could not you look before you, and be d---d? Do you think I have nothing else to do (in the devil's name) but to mend and repair after you?" "Good words, friend," said the bee, having now pruned himself, and being disposed to droll; "I'll give you my hand and word to come near your kennel no more; I was never in such a confounded pickle since I was born." "Sirrah," replied the spider, "if it were not for breaking an old custom in our family, never to stir abroad against an enemy, I should come and teach you better manners." "I pray have patience," said the bee, "or you'll spend your substance, and, for aught I see, you may stand in need of it all, towards the repair of your house." "Rogue, rogue," replied the spider, "yet methinks you should have more respect to a person whom all the world allows to be so much your betters." "By my troth," said the bee, "the comparison will amount to a very good jest, and you will do me a favour to let me know the reasons that all the world is pleased to use in so hopeful a dispute." At this the spider, having swelled himself into the size and posture of a disputant, began his argument in the true spirit of controversy, with resolution to be heartily scurrilous and angry, to urge on his own reasons without the least regard to the answers or objections of his opposite, and fully predetermined in his mind against all conviction.

"Not to disparage myself," said he, "by the comparison with such a rascal, what art thou but a vagabond without house or home, without stock or inheritance? born to no possession of your own, but a pair of wings and a drone-pipe. Your livelihood is a universal plunder upon nature; a freebooter over fields and gardens; and, for the sake of stealing, will rob a nettle as easily as a violet. Whereas I am a domestic animal, furnished with a native stock within myself. This large castle (to show my improvements in the mathematics) is all built with my own hands, and the materials extracted altogether out of my own person."

"I am glad," answered the bee, "to hear you grant at least that I am come honestly by my wings and my voice; for then, it seems, I am obliged to Heaven alone for my flights and my music; and Providence would never have bestowed on me two such gifts without designing them for the noblest ends. I visit, indeed, all the flowers and blossoms of the field and garden, but whatever I collect thence enriches myself without the least injury to their beauty, their smell, or their taste. Now, for you and your skill in architecture and other mathematics, I have little to say: in that building of yours there might, for aught I know, have been labour and method enough; but, by woeful experience for us both, it is too plain the materials are naught; and I hope you will henceforth take warning, and consider duration and matter, as well as method and art. You boast, indeed, of being obliged to no other creature, but of drawing and spinning out all from yourself; that is to say, if we may judge of the liquor in the vessel by what issues out, you possess a good plentiful store of dirt and poison in your breast; and, though I would by no means lesson or disparage your genuine stock of either, yet I doubt you are somewhat obliged, for an increase of both, to a little foreign assistance. Your inherent portion of dirt does not fall of acquisitions, by sweepings exhaled from below; and one insect furnishes you with a share of poison to destroy another. So that, in short, the question comes all to this: whether is the nobler being of the two, that which, by a lazy contemplation of four inches round, by an overweening pride, feeding, and engendering on itself, turns all into excrement and venom, producing nothing at all but flybane and a cobweb; or that which, by a universal range, with long search, much study, true judgment, and distinction of things, brings home honey and wax."

This dispute was managed with such eagerness, clamour, and warmth, that the two parties of books, in arms below, stood silent a while, waiting in suspense what would be the issue; which was not long undetermined: for the bee, grown impatient at so much loss of time, fled straight away to a bed of roses, without looking for a reply, and left the spider, like an orator, collected in himself, and just prepared to burst out.

It happened upon this emergency that AEsop broke silence first. He had been of late most barbarously treated by a strange effect of the regent's humanity, who had torn off his title-page, sorely defaced one half of his leaves, and chained him fast among a shelf of Moderns. Where, soon discovering how high the quarrel was likely to proceed, he tried all his arts, and turned himself to a thousand forms. At length, in the borrowed shape of an ass, the regent mistook him for a Modern; by which means he had time and opportunity to escape to the Ancients, just when the spider and the bee were entering into their contest; to which he gave his attention with a world of pleasure, and, when it was ended, swore in the loudest key that in all his life he had never known two cases, so parallel and adapt to each other as that in the window and this upon the shelves. "The disputants," said he, "have admirably managed the dispute between them, have taken in the full strength of all that is to be said on both sides, and exhausted the substance of every argument *pro* and *con*. It is but to adjust the reasonings of both to the present quarrel, then to compare and apply the labours and fruits of each, as the bee has learnedly deduced them, and we shall find the conclusion fall plain and close upon the Moderns and us. For pray, gentlemen, was ever anything so modern as the spider in his air, his turns, and his paradoxes? he argues in the behalf of you, his brethren, and himself, with many boastings of his native stock and great genius; that he spins and spits wholly from himself, and scorns to own any obligation or assistance from without. Then he displays to you his great skill in architecture and improvement in the mathematics. To all this the bee, as an advocate retained by us, the Ancients, thinks fit to answer, that, if one may judge of the great genius or inventions of the Moderns by what they have produced, you will hardly have countenance to bear you out in boasting of either. Erect your schemes with as much method and skill as you please; yet, if the materials be nothing but dirt, spun out of your own entrails (the guts of modern brains), the edifice will conclude at last in a cobweb; the duration of which, like that of other spiders' webs, may be imputed to their being forgotten, or neglected, or hid in a corner. For anything else of genuine that the Moderns may pretend to, I cannot recollect; unless it be a large vein of wrangling and satire, much of a nature and substance with the spiders' poison; which, however they pretend to spit wholly out of themselves, is improved by the same arts, by feeding upon the insects and vermin of the age. As for us, the Ancients, we are content with the bee, to pretend to nothing of our own beyond our wings and our voice: that is to say, our flights and our language. For the rest, whatever we have got has been by infinite labour and search, and ranging through every corner of nature; the difference is, that, instead of dirt and poison, we have rather chosen to till our hives with honey and wax; thus furnishing mankind with the two noblest of things, which are sweetness and light."

It is wonderful to conceive the tumult arisen among the books upon the close of this long descant of AEsop: both parties took the hint, and heightened their animosities so on a sudden, that they resolved it should come to a battle. Immediately the two main bodies withdrew, under their several ensigns, to the farther parts of the library, and there entered into cabals and consults upon the present emergency. The Moderns were in very warm debates upon the choice of their leaders;

and nothing less than the fear impending from their enemies could have kept them from mutinies upon this occasion. The difference was greatest among the horse, where every private trooper pretended to the chief command, from Tasso and Milton to Dryden and Wither. The light-horse were commanded by Cowley and Despreaux. There came the bowmen under their valiant leaders, Descartes, Gassendi, and Hobbes; whose strength was such that they could shoot their arrows beyond the atmosphere, never to fall down again, but turn, like that of Evander, into meteors; or, like the cannon-ball, into stars. Paracelsus brought a squadron of stinkpot-flingers from the snowy mountains of Rhaetia. There came a vast body of dragoons, of different nations, under the leading of Harvey, their great aga: part armed with scythes, the weapons of death; part with lances and long knives, all steeped in poison; part shot bullets of a most malignant nature, and used white powder, which infallibly killed without report. There came several bodies of heavy-armed foot, all mercenaries, under the ensigns of Guicciardini, Davila, Polydore Vergil, Buchanan, Mariana, Camden, and others. The engineers were commanded by Regiomontanus and Wilkins. The rest was a confused multitude, led by Scotus, Aquinas, and Bellarmine; of mighty bulk and stature, but without either arms, courage, or discipline. In the last place came infinite swarms of calones, a disorderly rout led by L'Estrange; rogues and ragamuffins, that follow the camp for nothing but the plunder, all without coats to cover them.

The army of the Ancients was much fewer in number; Homer led the horse, and Pindar the light-horse; Euclid was chief engineer; Plato and Aristotle commanded the bowmen; Herodotus and Livy the foot; Hippocrates, the dragoons; the allies, led by Vossius and Temple, brought up the rear.

All things violently tending to a decisive battle, Fame, who much frequented, and had a large apartment formerly assigned her in the regal library, fled up straight to Jupiter, to whom she delivered a faithful account of all that passed between the two parties below; for among the gods she always tells truth. Jove, in great concern, convokes a council in the Milky Way. The senate assembled, he declares the occasion of convening them; a bloody battle just impendent between two mighty armies of ancient and modern creatures, called books, wherein the celestial interest was but too deeply concerned. Momus, the patron of the Moderns, made an excellent speech in their favour, which was answered by Pallas, the protectress of the Ancients. The assembly was divided in their affections; when Jupiter commanded the Book of Fate to be laid before him. Immediately were brought by Mercury three large volumes in folio, containing memoirs of all things past, present, and to come. The clasps were of silver double gilt, the covers of celestial turkey leather, and the paper such as here on earth might pass almost for vellum. Jupiter, having silently read the decree, would communicate the import to none, but presently shut up the book.

Without the doors of this assembly there attended a vast number of light, nimble gods, menial servants to Jupiter: those are his ministering instruments in all affairs below. They travel in a caravan, more or less together, and are fastened to each other like a link of galley-slaves, by a light chain, which passes from them to Jupiter's great toe: and yet, in receiving or delivering a message, they may never approach above the lowest step of his throne, where he and they whisper to each other through a large hollow trunk. These deities are called by mortal men accidents or events; but the gods call them second causes. Jupiter having delivered his message to a certain number of these divinities, they flew immediately down to the pinnacle of the regal library, and consulting a few minutes, entered unseen, and disposed the parties according to their orders.

Meanwhile Momus, fearing the worst, and calling to mind an ancient prophecy which bore no very good face to his children the Moderns, bent his flight to the region of a malignant deity called Criticism. She dwelt on the top of a snowy mountain in Nova Zembla; there Momus found her extended in her den, upon the spoils of numberless volumes, half devoured. At her right hand sat Ignorance, her father and husband, blind with age; at her left, Pride, her mother, dressing her up in the scraps of paper herself had torn. There was Opinion, her sister, light of foot, hood-winked, and head-strong, yet giddy and perpetually turning. About her played her children, Noise and Impudence, Dulness and Vanity, Positiveness, Pedantry, and Ill-manners. The goddess herself had claws like a cat; her head, and ears, and voice resembled those of an ass; her teeth fallen out before, her eyes turned inward, as if she looked only upon herself; her diet was the overflowing of her own gall; her spleen was so large as to stand prominent, like a dug of the first rate; nor wanted excrescences in form of teats, at which a crew of ugly monsters were greedily sucking; and, what is wonderful to conceive, the bulk of spleen increased faster than the sucking could diminish it. "Goddess," said Momus, "can you sit idly here while our devout worshippers, the Moderns, are this minute entering into a cruel battle, and perhaps now lying under the swords of their enemies? who then hereafter will ever sacrifice or build altars to our divinities? Haste, therefore, to the British Isle, and, if possible, prevent their destruction; while I make factions among the gods, and gain them over to our party."

Momus, having thus delivered himself, stayed not for an answer, but left the goddess to her own resentment. Up she rose in a rage, and, as it is the form on such occasions, began a soliloquy: "It is I" (said she) "who give wisdom to infants and idiots; by me children grow wiser than their parents, by me beaux become politicians, and schoolboys judges of philosophy; by me sophisters debate and conclude upon the depths of knowledge; and coffee-house wits, instinct by me, can correct an author's style, and display his minutest errors, without understanding a syllable of his matter or his language; by me striplings spend their judgment, as they do their estate, before it comes into their hands. It is I who have deposed wit and knowledge from their empire over poetry, and advanced myself in their stead. And shall a few upstart Ancients dare to oppose me? But come, my aged parent, and you, my children dear, and thou, my beauteous sister; let us ascend my chariot, and haste to assist our devout Moderns, who are now sacrificing to us a hecatomb, as I perceive by that grateful smell which from thence reaches my nostrils."

The goddess and her train, having mounted the chariot, which was drawn by tame geese, flew over infinite regions, shedding her influence in due places, till at length she arrived at her beloved island of Britain; but in hovering over its metropolis, what blessings did she not let fall upon her seminaries of Gresham and Covent-garden! And now she reached the fatal plain of St. James's library, at what time the two armies were upon the point to engage; where, entering with all her caravan unseen, and landing upon a case of shelves, now desert, but once inhabited by a colony of virtuosos, she stayed awhile to observe the posture of both armies.

But here the tender cares of a mother began to fill her thoughts and move in her breast: for at the head of a troup of Modern bowmen she cast her eyes upon her son Wotton, to whom the fates had assigned a very short thread. Wotton, a young hero, whom an unknown father of mortal race begot by stolen embraces with this goddess. He was the darling of his mother above all her children, and she resolved to go and comfort him. But first, according to the good old custom of deities, she cast about to change her shape, for fear the divinity of her countenance might dazzle his mortal sight and overcharge the rest of his senses. She therefore gathered up her person into an octavo compass: her body grow white and arid, and split in pieces with dryness; the thick turned into pasteboard, and the thin into paper; upon which her parents and children artfully strewed a black juice, or decoction of gall and soot, in form of letters: her head, and voice, and spleen, kept their primitive form; and that which before was a cover of skin did still continue so. In this guise she marched on towards the Moderns, indistinguishable in shape and dress from the divine Bentley, Wotton's dearest friend. "Brave Wotton," said the goddess, "why do our troops stand idle here, to spend their present vigour and opportunity of the day? away, let us haste to the generals, and advise to give the onset immediately." Having spoke thus, she took the ugliest of her monsters, full glutted from her spleen, and flung it invisibly into his mouth, which, flying straight up into his head, squeezed out his eye-balls, gave him a distorted look, and half-overturned his brain. Then she privately ordered two of her beloved children, Dulness and Ill-manners, closely to attend his person in all encounters. Having thus accoutred him, she vanished in a mist, and the hero perceived it was the goddess his mother.

The destined hour of fate being now arrived, the fight began; whereof, before I dare adventure to make a particular description, I must, after the example of other authors, petition for a hundred tongues, and mouths, and hands, and pens, which would all be too little to perform so immense a work. Say, goddess, that presidest over history, who it was that first advanced in the field of battle! Paracelsus, at the head of his dragoons, observing Galen in the adverse wing, darted his javelin with a mighty force, which the brave Ancient received upon his shield, the point breaking in the second fold . . . *Hic pauca . . . . desunt* They bore the wounded aga on their shields to his chariot . . . *Desunt . . . nonnulla* . . . .

Then Aristotle, observing Bacon advance with a furious mien, drew his bow to the head, and let fly his arrow, which missed the valiant Modern and went whizzing over his head; but Descartes it hit; the steel point quickly found a defect in his head-piece; it pierced the leather and the pasteboard, and went in at his right eye. The torture of the pain whirled the valiant bow-man round till death, like a star of superior influence, drew him into his own vortex *Ingens hiatus . . . . hic in MS.* .

. . . . . . . when Homer appeared at the head of the cavalry, mounted on a furious horse, with difficulty managed by the rider himself, but which no other mortal durst approach; he rode among the enemy's ranks, and bore down all before him. Say, goddess, whom he slew first and whom he slew last! First, Gondibert advanced against him, clad in heavy armour and mounted on a staid sober gelding, not so famed for his speed as his docility in kneeling whenever his rider would mount or alight. He had made a vow to Pallas that he would never leave the field till he had spoiled Homer of his armour: madman, who had never once seen the wearer, nor understood his strength! Him Homer overthrew, horse and man, to the ground, there to be trampled and choked in the dirt. Then with a long spear he slew Denham, a stout Modern, who from his father's side derived his lineage from Apollo, but his mother was of mortal race. He fell, and bit the earth. The celestial part Apollo took, and made it a star; but the terrestrial lay wallowing upon the ground. Then Homer slew Sam Wesley with a kick of his horse's heel; he took Perrault by mighty force out of his saddle, then hurled him at Fontenelle, with the same blow dashing out both their brains.

On the left wing of the horse Virgil appeared, in shining armour, completely fitted to his body; he was mounted on a dapple-grey steed, the slowness of whose pace was an effect of the highest mettle and vigour. He cast his eye on the adverse wing, with a desire to find an object worthy of his valour, when behold upon a sorrel gelding of a monstrous size appeared a foe, issuing from among the thickest of the enemy's squadrons; but his speed was less than his noise; for his horse, old and lean, spent the dregs of his strength in a high trot, which, though it made slow advances, yet caused a loud clashing of his armour, terrible to hear. The two cavaliers had now approached within the throw of a lance, when the stranger desired a parley, and, lifting up the visor of his helmet, a face hardly appeared from within which, after a pause, was known for that of the renowned Dryden. The brave Ancient suddenly started, as one possessed with surprise and disappointment together; for the helmet was nine times too large for the head, which appeared situate far in the hinder part, even like the lady in a lobster, or like a mouse under a canopy of state, or like a shrivelled beau from within the penthouse of a modern periwig; and the voice was suited to the visage, sounding weak and remote. Dryden, in a long harangue, soothed up the good Ancient; called him father, and, by a large deduction of genealogies, made it plainly appear that they were nearly related. Then he humbly proposed an exchange of armour, as a lasting mark of hospitality between them. Virgil consented (for the goddess Diffidence came unseen, and cast a mist before his eyes), though his was of gold and cost a hundred beeves, the other's but of rusty iron. However, this glittering armour became the Modern yet worsen than his own. Then they agreed to exchange horses; but, when it came to the trial, Dryden was afraid and utterly unable to mount. . . ***Alter hiatus*** . . . . ***in MS.*** Lucan appeared upon a fiery horse of admirable shape, but headstrong, bearing the rider where he list over the field; he made a mighty slaughter among the enemy's horse; which destruction to stop, Blackmore, a famous Modern (but one of the mercenaries), strenuously opposed himself, and darted his javelin with a strong hand, which, falling short of its mark, struck deep in the earth. Then Lucan threw a lance; but AEsculapius came unseen and turned off the point. "Brave Modern," said Lucan, "I perceive some god protects you, for never did my arm so deceive me before: but what mortal can contend with a god? Therefore, let us fight no longer, but present gifts to each other." Lucan then bestowed on the Modern a pair of spurs, and Blackmore gave Lucan a bridle. . . . ***Pauca desunt*** . . . . . . . . Creech: but the goddess Dulness took a cloud, formed into the shape of Horace, armed and mounted, and placed in a flying posture before him. Glad was the cavalier to begin a combat with a flying foe, and pursued the image, threatening aloud; till at last it led him to the peaceful bower of his father, Ogleby, by whom he was disarmed and assigned to his repose.

Then Pindar slew ---, and --- and Oldham, and ---, and Afra the Amazon, light of foot; never advancing in a direct line, but wheeling with incredible agility and force, he made a terrible slaughter among the enemy's light-horse. Him when Cowley observed, his generous heart burnt within him, and he advanced against the fierce Ancient, imitating his address, his pace, and career, as well as the vigour of his horse and his own skill would allow. When the two cavaliers had approached within the length of three javelins, first Cowley threw a lance, which missed Pindar, and, passing into the enemy's ranks, fell ineffectual to the ground. Then Pindar darted a javelin so large and weighty, that scarce a dozen Cavaliers, as cavaliers are in our degenerate days, could raise it from the ground; yet he threw it with ease, and it went, by an unerring hand, singing through the air; nor could the Modern have avoided present death if he had not luckily opposed the shield that had been given him by Venus. And now both heroes drew their swords; but the Modern was so aghast and disordered that he knew not where he was; his shield dropped from his hands; thrice he fled, and thrice he could not escape. At last he turned, and lifting up his hand in the posture of a suppliant, "Godlike Pindar," said he, "spare my life, and possess my horse, with these arms, beside the ransom which my friends will give when they hear I am alive and your prisoner." "Dog!" said Pindar, "let your ransom stay with your friends; but your carcase shall be left for the fowls of the air and the beasts of the field." With that he raised his sword, and, with a mighty stroke, cleft the wretched Modern in twain, the sword pursuing the blow; and one half lay panting on the ground, to be trod in pieces by the horses' feet; the other half was borne by the frighted steed through the field. This Venus took, washed it seven times in ambrosia, then struck it thrice with a sprig of amaranth; upon which the leather grow round and soft, and the leaves turned into feathers, and, being gilded before, continued gilded still; so it became a dove, and she harnessed it to her chariot. . . . . . . . *Hiatus valde de-* . . . . *flendus in MS*.

# THE EPISODE OF BENTLEY AND WOTTON.

Day being far spent, and the numerous forces of the Moderns half inclining to a retreat, there issued forth, from a squadron of their heavy-armed foot, a captain whose name was Bentley, the most deformed of all the Moderns; tall, but without shape or comeliness; large, but without strength or proportion. His armour was patched up of a thousand incoherent pieces, and the sound of it, as he marched, was loud and dry, like that made by the fall of a sheet of lead, which an Etesian wind blows suddenly down from the roof of some steeple. His helmet was of old rusty iron, but the vizor was brass, which, tainted by his breath, corrupted into copperas, nor wanted gall from the same fountain, so that, whenever provoked by anger or labour, an atramentous quality, of most malignant nature, was seen to distil from his lips. In his right hand he grasped a flail, and (that he might never be unprovided of an offensive weapon) a vessel full of ordure in his left. Thus completely armed, he advanced with a slow and heavy pace where the Modern chiefs were holding a consult upon the sum of things, who, as he came onwards, laughed to behold his crooked leg and humped shoulder, which his boot and armour, vainly endeavouring to hide, were forced to comply with and expose. The generals made use of him for his talent of railing, which, kept within government, proved frequently of great service to their cause, but, at other times, did more mischief than good; for, at the least touch of offence, and often without any at all, he would, like a wounded elephant, convert it against his leaders. Such, at this juncture, was the disposition of Bentley, grieved to see the enemy prevail, and dissatisfied with everybody's conduct but his own. He humbly gave the Modern generals to understand that he conceived, with great submission, they were all a pack of rogues, and fools, and confounded logger-heads, and illiterate whelps, and nonsensical scoundrels; that, if himself had been constituted general, those presumptuous dogs, the Ancients, would long before this have been beaten out of the field. "You," said he, "sit here idle, but when I, or any other valiant Modern kill an enemy, you are sure to seize the spoil. But I will not march one foot against the foe till you all swear to me that whomever I take or kill, his arms I shall quietly possess." Bentley having spoken thus, Scaliger, bestowing him a sour look, "Miscreant prater!" said he, "eloquent only in thine own eyes, thou railest without wit, or truth, or discretion. The malignity of thy temper perverteth nature; thy learning makes thee more barbarous; thy study of humanity more inhuman; thy converse among poets more grovelling, miry, and dull. All arts of civilising others render thee rude and untractable; courts have taught thee ill manners, and polite conversation has finished thee a pedant. Besides, a greater coward burdeneth not the army. But never despond; I pass my word, whatever spoil thou takest shall certainly be thy own; though I hope that vile carcase will first become a prey to kites and worms."

Bentley durst not reply, but, half choked with spleen and rage, withdrew, in full resolution of performing some great achievement. With him, for his aid and companion, he took his beloved Wotton, resolving by policy or surprise to attempt some neglected quarter of the Ancients' army. They began their march over carcases of their slaughtered friends; then to the right of their own forces; then wheeled northward, till they came to Aldrovandus's tomb, which they passed on the side of the declining sun. And now they arrived, with fear, toward the enemy's out-guards, looking about, if haply they might spy the quarters of the wounded, or some straggling sleepers, unarmed and remote from the rest. As when two mongrel curs, whom native greediness and domestic want provoke and join in partnership, though fearful, nightly to invade the folds of some rich grazier, they, with tails depressed and lolling tongues, creep soft and slow. Meanwhile the conscious moon, now in her zenith, on their guilty heads darts perpendicular rays; nor dare they bark, though much provoked at her refulgent visage, whether seen in puddle by reflection or in sphere direct; but one surveys the region round, while the other scouts the plain, if haply to discover, at distance from the flock, some carcase half devoured, the refuse of gorged wolves or ominous ravens. So marched this lovely, loving pair of friends, nor with less fear and circumspection, when at a distance they might perceive two shining suits of armour hanging upon an oak, and the owners not far off in a profound sleep. The two friends drew lots, and the pursuing of this adventure fell to Bentley; on he went, and in his van Confusion and Amaze, while Horror and Affright brought up the rear. As he came near, behold two heroes of the Ancient army, Phalaris and Æsop, lay fast asleep. Bentley would fain have despatched them both, and, stealing close, aimed his flail at Phalaris's breast; but then the goddess Affright, interposing, caught the Modern in her icy arms, and dragged him from the danger she foresaw; both the dormant heroes happened to turn at the same instant, though soundly sleeping, and busy in a dream. For Phalaris was just that minute dreaming how a most vile poetaster had lampooned him, and how he had got him roaring in his bull. And Æsop dreamed that as he and the Ancient were lying on the ground, a wild ass broke loose, ran about, trampling and kicking in their faces. Bentley, leaving the two heroes asleep, seized on both their armours, and withdrew in quest of his darling Wotton.

He, in the meantime, had wandered long in search of some enterprise, till at length he arrived at a small rivulet that issued from a fountain hard by, called, in the language of mortal men, Helicon. Here he stopped, and, parched with thirst, resolved to allay it in this limpid stream. Thrice with profane hands he essayed to raise the water to his lips, and thrice it slipped all through his fingers. Then he stopped prone on his breast, but, ere his mouth had kissed the liquid crystal, Apollo came, and in the channel held his shield betwixt the Modern and the fountain, so that he drew up nothing but mud. For, although no fountain on earth can compare with the clearness of Helicon, yet there lies at bottom a thick sediment of slime and mud; for so Apollo begged of Jupiter, as a punishment to those who durst attempt to taste it with unhallowed lips, and for a lesson to all not to draw too deep or far from the spring.

At the fountain-head Wotton discerned two heroes; the one he could not distinguish, but the other was soon known for Temple, general of the allies to the Ancients. His back was turned, and he was employed in drinking large draughts in his helmet from the fountain, where he had withdrawn himself to rest from the toils of the war. Wotton, observing him, with quaking knees and trembling hands, spoke thus to himself: O that I could kill this destroyer of our army, what renown should I purchase among the chiefs! but to issue out against him, man against man, shield against shield, and lance against lance, what Modern of us dare? for he fights like a god, and Pallas or Apollo are ever at his elbow. But, O mother! if what Fame reports be true, that I am the son of so great a goddess, grant me to hit Temple with this lance, that the stroke may send him to hell, and that I may return in safety and triumph, laden with his spoils. The first part of this prayer the gods granted at the intercession of his mother and of Momus; but the rest, by a perverse wind sent from Fate, was scattered in the air. Then Wotton grasped his lance, and, brandishing it thrice over his head, darted it with all his might; the goddess, his mother, at the same time adding strength to his arm. Away the lance went hizzing, and reached even to the belt of the averted Ancient, upon which, lightly grazing, it fell to the ground. Temple neither felt the weapon touch him nor heard it fall: and Wotton might have escaped to his army, with the honour of having remitted his lance against so great a leader unrevenged; but Apollo, enraged that a javelin flung by the assistance of so foul a goddess should pollute his fountain, put on the shape of ---, and softly came to young Boyle, who then accompanied Temple: he pointed first to the lance, then to the distant Modern that flung it, and commanded the young hero to take immediate revenge. Boyle, clad in a suit of armour which had been given him by all the gods, immediately advanced against the trembling foe, who now fled before him. As a young lion in the Libyan plains, or Araby desert, sent by his aged sire to hunt for prey, or health, or exercise, he scours along, wishing to meet some tiger from the mountains, or a furious boar; if chance a wild ass, with brayings importune, affronts his ear, the generous beast, though loathing to distain his claws with blood so vile, yet, much provoked at the offensive noise, which Echo, foolish nymph, like her ill-judging sex, repeats much louder, and with more delight than Philomela's song, he vindicates the honour of the forest, and hunts the noisy long-eared animal. So Wotton fled, so Boyle pursued. But Wotton, heavy-armed, and slow of foot, began to slack his course, when his lover Bentley appeared, returning laden with the spoils of the two sleeping Ancients. Boyle observed him well, and soon discovering the helmet and shield of Phalaris his friend, both which he had lately with his own hands new polished and gilt, rage sparkled in his eyes, and, leaving his pursuit after Wotton, he furiously rushed on against this new approacher. Fain would he be revenged on both; but both now fled different ways: and, as a woman in a little house that gets a painful livelihood by spinning, if chance her geese be scattered o'er the common, she courses round the plain from side to side, compelling here and there the stragglers to the flock; they cackle loud, and flutter o'er the champaign; so Boyle pursued, so fled this pair of friends: finding at length their flight was vain, they bravely joined, and drew themselves in phalanx. First Bentley threw a spear with all his force, hoping to pierce the enemy's breast; but Pallas came unseen, and in the air took off the point, and clapped on one of lead, which, after a dead bang against the enemy's shield, fell blunted to the ground. Then Boyle, observing well his time, took up a lance of wondrous length and sharpness; and, as this pair of friends compacted, stood close side by side, he wheeled him to the right, and, with unusual force, darted the weapon. Bentley saw his fate approach, and flanking down his arms close to his ribs, hoping to save his body, in went the point, passing through arm and side, nor stopped or spent its force till it had also pierced the valiant Wotton, who, going to sustain his dying friend, shared his fate. As when a skilful cook has trussed a brace of woodcocks, he with iron skewer pierces the tender sides of both, their legs and wings close pinioned to the rib; so was this pair of friends transfixed, till down they fell, joined in their lives, joined in their deaths; so closely joined that Charon would mistake them both for one, and waft them over Styx for half his fare. Farewell, beloved, loving pair; few equals have you left behind: and happy and immortal shall you be, if all my wit and eloquence can make you.

And now. . . .

***Desunt coetera.***

# A MEDITATION UPON A BROOMSTICK.

*According to the Style and Manner of the Hon. Robert Boyle's Meditations*.

This single stick, which you now behold ingloriously lying in that neglected corner, I once knew in a flourishing state in a forest. It was full of sap, full of leaves, and full of boughs; but now in vain does the busy art of man pretend to vie with nature, by tying that withered bundle of twigs to its sapless trunk; it is now at best but the reverse of what it was, a tree turned upside-down, the branches on the earth, and the root in the air; it is now handled by every dirty wench, condemned to do her drudgery, and, by a capricious kind of fate, destined to make other things clean, and be nasty itself; at length, worn to the stumps in the service of the maids, it is either thrown out of doors or condemned to the last use--of kindling a fire. When I behold this I sighed, and said within myself, "Surely mortal man is a broomstick!" Nature sent him into the world strong and lusty, in a thriving condition, wearing his own hair on his head, the proper branches of this reasoning vegetable, till the axe of intemperance has lopped off his green boughs, and left him a withered trunk; he then flies to art, and puts on a periwig, valuing himself upon an unnatural bundle of hairs, all covered with powder, that never grew on his head; but now should this our broomstick pretend to enter the scene, proud of those birchen spoils it never bore, and all covered with dust, through the sweepings of the finest lady's chamber, we should be apt to ridicule and despise its vanity. Partial judges that we are of our own excellencies, and other men's defaults!

But a broomstick, perhaps you will say, is an emblem of a tree standing on its head; and pray what is a man but a topsy-turvy creature, his animal faculties perpetually mounted on his rational, his head where his heels should be, grovelling on the earth? And yet, with all his faults, he sets up to be a universal reformer and corrector of abuses, a remover of grievances, rakes into every slut's corner of nature, bringing hidden corruptions to the light, and raises a mighty dust where there was none before, sharing deeply all the while in the very same pollutions he pretends to sweep away. His last days are spent in slavery to women, and generally the least deserving; till, worn to the stumps, like his brother besom, he is either kicked out of doors, or made use of to kindle flames for others to warm themselves by.

# PREDICTIONS FOR THE YEAR 1708.

WHEREIN THE MONTH, AND DAY OF THE MONTH ARE SET DOWN, THE PERSONS NAMED, AND THE GREAT ACTIONS AND EVENTS OF NEXT YEAR PARTICULARLY RELATED AS WILL COME TO PASS.

*Written to prevent the people of England from being farther imposed on by vulgar Almanack-makers*.

BY ISAAC BICKERSTAFF, ESQ.

I have long considered the gross abuse of astrology in this kingdom, and upon debating the matter with myself, I could not possibly lay the fault upon the art, but upon those gross impostors who set up to be the artists. I know several learned men have contended that the whole is a cheat; that it is absurd and ridiculous to imagine the stars can have any influence at all upon human actions, thoughts, or inclinations; and whoever has not bent his studies that way may be excused for thinking so, when he sees in how wretched a manner that noble art is treated by a few mean illiterate traders between us and the stars, who import a yearly stock of nonsense, lies, folly, and impertinence, which they offer to the world as genuine from the planets, though they descend from no greater a height than their own brains.

I intend in a short time to publish a large and rational defence of this art, and therefore shall say no more in its justification at present than that it hath been in all ages defended by many learned men, and among the rest by Socrates himself, whom I look upon as undoubtedly the wisest of uninspired mortals: to which if we add that those who have condemned this art, though otherwise learned, having been such as either did not apply their studies this way, or at least did not succeed in their applications, their testimony will not be of much weight to its disadvantage, since they are liable to the common objection of condemning what they did not understand.

Nor am I at all offended, or think it an injury to the art, when I see the common dealers in it, the students in astrology, the Philomaths, and the rest of that tribe, treated by wise men with the utmost scorn and contempt; but rather wonder, when I observe gentlemen in the country, rich enough to serve the nation in Parliament, poring in Partridge's Almanack to find out the events of the year at home and abroad, not daring to propose a hunting-match till Gadbury or he have fixed the weather.

I will allow either of the two I have mentioned, or any other of the fraternity, to be not only astrologers, but conjurers too, if I do not produce a hundred instances in all their almanacks to convince any reasonable man that they do not so much as understand common grammar and syntax; that they are not able to spell any word out of the usual road, nor even in their prefaces write common sense or intelligible English. Then for their observations and predictions, they are such as will equally suit any age or country in the world. "This month a certain great person will be threatened with death or sickness." This the newspapers will tell them; for there we find at the end of the year that no month passes without the death of some person of note; and it would be hard if it should be otherwise, when there are at least two thousand persons of note in this kingdom, many of them old, and the almanack-maker has the liberty of choosing the sickliest season of the year where he may fix his prediction. Again, "This month an eminent clergyman will be preferred;" of which there may be some hundreds, half of them with one foot in the grave. Then "such a planet in such a house shows great machinations, plots, and conspiracies, that may in time be brought to light:" after which, if we hear of any discovery, the astrologer gets the honour; if not, his prediction still stands good. And at last, "God preserve King William from all his open and secret enemies, Amen." When if the King should happen to have died, the astrologer plainly foretold it; otherwise it passes but for the pious ejaculation of a loyal subject; though it unluckily happened in some of their almanacks that poor King William was prayed for many months after he was dead, because it fell out that he died about the beginning of the year.

To mention no more of their impertinent predictions: what have we to do with their advertisements about pills and drink for disease? or their mutual quarrels in verse and prose of Whig and Tory, wherewith the stars have little to do?

Having long observed and lamented these, and a hundred other abuses of this art, too tedious to repeat, I resolved to proceed in a new way, which I doubt not will be to the general satisfaction of the kingdom. I can this year produce but a specimen of what I design for the future, having employed most part of my time in adjusting and correcting the calculations I made some years past, because I would offer nothing to the world of which I am not as fully satisfied as that I am now alive. For these two last years I have not failed in above one or two particulars, and those of no very great moment. I exactly foretold the miscarriage at Toulon, with all its particulars, and the loss of Admiral Shovel, though I was mistaken as to the day, placing that accident about thirty-six hours sooner than it happened; but upon reviewing my schemes, I quickly found the cause of that error. I likewise foretold the Battle of Almanza to the very day and hour, with the lose on both sides, and the consequences thereof. All which I showed to some friends many months before they happened--that is, I gave them papers sealed up, to open at such a time, after which they were at liberty to read them; and there they found my predictions true in every article, except one or two very minute.

As for the few following predictions I now offer the world, I forbore to publish them till I had perused the several almanacks for the year we are now entered on. I find them all in the usual strain, and I beg the reader will compare their manner with mine. And here I make bold to tell the world that I lay the whole credit of my art upon the truth of these predictions; and I will be content that Partridge, and the rest of his clan, may hoot me for a cheat and impostor if I fail in any single particular of moment. I believe any man who reads this paper will look upon me to be at least a person of as much honesty and understanding as a common maker of almanacks. I do not lurk in the dark; I am not wholly unknown in the world; I have set my name at length, to be a mark of infamy to mankind, if they shall find I deceive them.

In one thing I must desire to be forgiven, that I talk more sparingly of home affairs. As it will be imprudence to discover secrets of State, so it would be danger-ous to my person; but in smaller matters, and that are not of public consequence, I shall be very free; and the truth of my conjectures will as much appear from those as the others. As for the most signal events abroad, in France, Flanders, Italy, and Spain, I shall make no scruple to predict them in plain terms. Some of them are of importance, and I hope I shall seldom mistake the day they will happen; therefore I think good to inform the reader that I all along make use of the Old Style observed in England, which I desire he will compare with that of the newspapers at the time they relate the actions I mention.

I must add one word more. I know it hath been the opinion of several of the learned, who think well enough of the true art of astrology, that the stars do only incline, and not force the actions or wills of men, and therefore, however I may proceed by right rules, yet I cannot in prudence so confidently assure the events will follow exactly as I predict them.

I hope I have maturely considered this objection, which in some cases is of no little weight. For example: a man may, by the influence of an over- ruling planet, be disposed or inclined to lust, rage, or avarice, and yet by the force of reason overcome that bad influence; and this was the case of Socrates. But as the great events of the world usually depend upon numbers of men, it cannot be expected they should all unite to cross their inclinations from pursuing a general design wherein they unanimously agree. Besides, the influence of the stars reaches to many actions and events which are not any way in the power of reason, as sickness, death, and what we commonly call accidents, with many more, needless to repeat.

But now it is time to proceed to my predictions, which I have begun to calculate from the time that the sun enters into Aries. And this I take to be properly the beginning of the natural year. I pursue them to the time that he enters Libra, or somewhat more, which is the busy period of the year. The remainder I have not yet adjusted, upon account of several impediments needless here to mention. Besides, I must remind the reader again that this is but a specimen of what I design in succeeding years to treat more at large, if I may have liberty and encouragement.

My first prediction is but a trifle, yet I will mention it, to show how ignorant those sottish pretenders to astrology are in their own concerns. It relates to Partridge, the almanack-maker. I have consulted the stars of his nativity by my own rules, and find he will infallibly die upon the 29th of March next, about eleven at night, of a raging fever; therefore I advise him to consider of it, and settle his affairs in time.

The month of *April* will be observable for the death of many great persons. On the 4th will die the Cardinal de Noailles, Archbishop of Paris; on the 11th, the young Prince of Asturias, son to the Duke of Anjou; on the 14th, a great peer of this realm will die at his country house; on the 19th, an old layman of great fame for learning, and on the 23rd, an eminent goldsmith in Lombard Street. I could mention others, both at home and abroad, if I did not consider it is of very little use or instruction to the reader, or to the world.

As to public affairs: On the 7th of this month there will be an insurrection in Dauphiny, occasioned by the oppressions of the people, which will not be quieted in some months.

On the 15th will be a violent storm on the south-east coast of France, which will destroy many of their ships, and some in the very harbour.

The 11th will be famous for the revolt of a whole province or kingdom, excepting one city, by which the affairs of a certain prince in the Alliance will take a better face.

*May*, against common conjectures, will be no very busy month in Europe, but very signal for the death of the Dauphin, which will happen on the 7th, after a short fit of sickness, and grievous torments with the strangury. He dies less lamented by the Court than the kingdom.

On the 9th a Marshal of France will break his leg by a fall from his horse. I have not been able to discover whether he will then die or not.

On the 11th will begin a most important siege, which the eyes of all Europe will be upon: I cannot be more particular, for in relating affairs that so nearly concern the Confederates, and consequently this kingdom, I am forced to confine myself for several reasons very obvious to the reader.

On the 15th news will arrive of a very surprising event, than which nothing could be more unexpected.

On the 19th three noble ladies of this kingdom will, against all expectation, prove with child, to the great joy of their husbands.

On the 23rd a famous buffoon of the playhouse will die a ridiculous death, suitable to his vocation.

*June*. This month will be distinguished at home by the utter dispersing of those ridiculous deluded enthusiasts commonly called the Prophets, occasioned chiefly by seeing the time come that many of their prophecies should be fulfilled, and then finding themselves deceived by contrary events. It is indeed to be admired how any deceiver can be so weak to foretell things near at hand, when a very few months must of necessity discover the impostor to all the world; in this point less prudent than common almanack-makers, who are so wise to wonder in generals, and talk dubiously, and leave to the reader the business of interpreting.

On the 1st of this month a French general will be killed by a random shot of a cannon-ball.

On the 6th a fire will break out in the suburbs of Paris, which will destroy above a thousand houses, and seems to be the foreboding of what will happen, to the surprise of all Europe, about the end of the following month.

On the 10th a great battle will be fought, which will begin at four of the clock in the afternoon, and last till nine at night with great obstinacy, but no very decisive event. I shall not name the place, for the reasons aforesaid, but the commanders on each left wing will be killed. I see bonfires and hear the noise of guns for a victory.

On the 14th there will be a false report of the French king's death.

On the 20th Cardinal Portocarero will die of a dysentery, with great suspicion of poison, but the report of his intention to revolt to King Charles will prove false.

*July*. The 6th of this month a certain general will, by a glorious action, recover the reputation he lost by former misfortunes.

On the 12th a great commander will die a prisoner in the hands of his enemies.

On the 14th a shameful discovery will be made of a French Jesuit giving poison to a great foreign general; and when he is put to the torture, will make wonderful discoveries.

In short, this will prove a month of great action, if I might have liberty to relate the particulars.

At home, the death of an old famous senator will happen on the 15th at his country house, worn with age and diseases.

But that which will make this month memorable to all posterity is the death of the French king, Louis the Fourteenth, after a week's sickness at Marli, which will happen on the 29th, about six o'clock in the evening. It seems to be an effect of the gout in his stomach, followed by a flux. And in three days after Monsieur Chamillard will follow his master, dying suddenly of an apoplexy.

In this month likewise an ambassador will die in London, but I cannot assign the day.

*August*. The affairs of France will seem to suffer no change for a while under the Duke of Burgundy's administration; but the genius that animated the whole machine being gone, will be the cause of mighty turns and revolutions in the following year. The new king makes yet little change either in the army or the Ministry, but the libels against his grandfather, that fly about his very Court, give him uneasiness.

I see an express in mighty haste, with joy and wonder in his looks, arriving by break of day on the 26th of this month, having travelled in three days a prodigious journey by land and sea. In the evening I hear bells and guns, and see the blazing of a thousand bonfires.

A young admiral of noble birth does likewise this month gain immortal honour by a great achievement.

The affairs of Poland are this month entirely settled; Augustus resigns his pretensions which he had again taken up for some time: Stanislaus is peaceably possessed of the throne, and the King of Sweden declares for the emperor.

I cannot omit one particular accident here at home: that near the end of this month much mischief will be done at Bartholomew Fair by the fall of a booth.

*September*. This month begins with a very surprising fit of frosty weather, which will last near twelve days.

The Pope, having long languished last month, the swellings in his legs breaking, and the flesh mortifying, will die on the 11th instant; and in three weeks' time, after a mighty contest, be succeeded by a cardinal of the Imperial faction, but native of Tuscany, who is now about sixty-one years old.

The French army acts now wholly on the defensive, strongly fortified in their trenches, and the young French king sends overtures for a treaty of peace by the Duke of Mantua; which, because it is a matter of State that concerns us here at home, I shall speak no farther of it.

I shall add but one prediction more, and that in mystical terms, which shall be included in a verse out of Virgil--

 *Alter erit jam Tethys*, *et altera quae vehat Argo*  *Delectos Heroas*.

Upon the 25th day of this month, the fulfilling of this prediction will be manifest to everybody.

This is the farthest I have proceeded in my calculations for the present year. I do not pretend that these are all the great events which will happen in this period, but that those I have set down will infallibly come to pass. It will perhaps still be objected why I have not spoken more particularly of affairs at home, or of the success of our armies abroad, which I might, and could very largely have done; but those in power have wisely discouraged men from meddling in public concerns, and I was resolved by no means to give the least offence. This I will venture to say, that it will be a glorious campaign for the Allies, wherein the English forces, both by sea and land, will have their full share of honour; that Her Majesty Queen Anne will continue in health and prosperity; and that no ill accident will arrive to any in the chief Ministry.

As to the particular events I have mentioned, the readers may judge by the fulfilling of them, whether I am on the level with common astrologers, who, with an old paltry cant, and a few pothooks for planets, to amuse the vulgar, have, in my opinion, too long been suffered to abuse the world. But an honest physician ought not to be despised because there are such things as mountebanks. I hope I have some share of reputation, which I would not willingly forfeit for a frolic or humour; and I believe no gentleman who reads this paper will look upon it to be of the same cast or mould with the common scribblers that are every day hawked about. My fortune has placed me above the little regard of scribbling for a few pence, which I neither value nor want; therefore, let no wise man too hastily condemn this essay, intended for a good design, to cultivate and improve an ancient art long in disgrace, by having fallen into mean and unskilful hands. A little time will determine whether I have deceived others or myself; and I think it is no very unreasonable request that men would please to suspend their judgments till then. I was once of the opinion with those who despise all predictions from the stars, till in the year 1686 a man of quality showed me, written in his album, that the most learned astronomer, Captain H---, assured him, he would never believe anything of the stars' influence if there were not a great revolution in England in the year 1688. Since that time I began to have other thoughts, and after eighteen years' diligent study and application, I think I have no reason to repent of my pains. I shall detain the reader no longer than to let him know that the account I design to give of next year's events shall take in the principal affairs that happen in Europe; and if I be denied the liberty of offering it to my own country, I shall appeal to the learned world, by publishing it in Latin, and giving order to have it printed in Holland.

## THE ACCOMPLISHMENT OF THE FIRST OF MR. BICKERSTAFF'S PREDICTIONS; BEING AN ACCOUNT OF THE DEATH OF MR. PARTRIDGE THE ALMANACK-MAKER, UPON THE 29TH INSTANT.

### *In a Letter to a Person of Honour*; *Written in the Year* 1708.

My Lord,--In obedience to your lordship's commands, as well as to satisfy my own curiosity, I have for some days past inquired constantly after Partridge the almanack-maker, of whom it was foretold in Mr. Bickerstaff's predictions, published about a month ago, that he should die the 29th instant, about eleven at night, of a raging fever. I had some sort of knowledge of him when I was employed in the Revenue, because he used every year to present me with his almanack, as he did other gentlemen, upon the score of some little gratuity we gave him. I saw him accidentally once or twice about ten days before he died, and observed he began very much to droop and languish, though I hear his friends did not seem to apprehend him in any danger. About two or three days ago he grew ill, was confined first to his chamber, and in a few hours after to his bed, where Dr. Case and Mrs. Kirleus were sent for, to visit and to prescribe to him. Upon this intelligence I sent thrice every day one servant or other to inquire after his health; and yesterday, about four in the afternoon, word was brought me that he was past hopes; upon which, I prevailed with myself to go and see him, partly out of commiseration, and I confess, partly out of curiosity. He knew me very well, seemed surprised at my condescension, and made me compliments upon it as well as he could in the condition he was. The people about him said he had been for some time delirious; but when I saw him, he had his understanding as well as ever I knew, and spoke strong and hearty, without any seeming uneasiness or constraint. After I had told him how sorry I was to see him in those melancholy circumstances, and said some other civilities suitable to the occasion, I desired him to tell me freely and ingenuously, whether the predictions Mr. Bickerstaff had published relating to his death had not too much affected and worked on his imagination. He confessed he had often had it in his head, but never with much apprehension, till about a fortnight before; since which time it had the perpetual possession of his mind and thoughts, and he did verily believe was the true natural cause of his present distemper: "For," said he, "I am thoroughly persuaded, and I think I have very good reasons, that Mr. Bickerstaff spoke altogether by guess, and knew no more what will happen this year than I did myself." I told him his discourse surprised me, and I would be glad he were in a state of health to be able to tell me what reason he had to be convinced of Mr. Bickerstaff's ignorance. He replied, "I am a poor, ignorant follow, bred to a mean trade, yet I have sense enough to know that all pretences of foretelling by astrology are deceits, for this manifest reason, because the wise and the learned, who can only know whether there be any truth in this science, do all unanimously agree to laugh at and despise it; and none but the poor ignorant vulgar give it any credit, and that only upon the word of such silly wretches as I and my fellows, who can hardly write or read." I then asked him why he had not calculated his own nativity, to see whether it agreed with Bickerstaff's prediction, at which he shook his head and said, "Oh, sir, this is no time for jesting, but for repenting those fooleries, as I do now from the very bottom of my heart." "By what I can gather from you," said I, "the observations and predictions you printed with your almanacks were mere impositions on the people." He replied, "If it were otherwise I should have the less to answer for. We have a common form for all those things; as to foretelling the weather, we never meddle with that, but leave it to the printer, who takes it out of any old almanack as he thinks fit; the rest was my own invention, to make my almanack sell, having a wife to maintain, and no other way to get my bread; for mending old shoes is a poor livelihood; and," added he, sighing, "I wish I may not have done more mischief by my physic than my astrology; though I had some good receipts from my grandmother, and my own compositions were such as I thought could at least do no hurt."

I had some other discourse with him, which now I cannot call to mind; and I fear I have already tired your lordship. I shall only add one circumstance, that on his death-bed he declared himself a Nonconformist, and had a fanatic preacher to be his spiritual guide. After half an hour's conversation I took my leave, being half stifled by the closeness of the room. I imagined he could not hold out long, and therefore withdrew to a little coffee-house hard by, leaving a servant at the house with orders to come immediately and tell me, as nearly as he could, the minute when Partridge should expire, which was not above two hours after, when, looking upon my watch, I found it to be above five minutes after seven; by which it is clear that Mr. Bickerstaff was mistaken almost four hours in his calculation. In the other circumstances he was exact enough. But, whether he has not been the cause of this poor man's death, as well as the predictor, may be very reasonably disputed. However, it must be confessed the matter is odd enough, whether we should endeavour to account for it by chance, or the effect of imagination. For my own part, though I believe no man has less faith in these matters, yet I shall wait with some impatience, and not without some expectation, the fulfilling of Mr. Bickerstaff's second prediction, that the Cardinal do Noailles is to die upon the 4th of April, and if that should be verified as exactly as this of poor Partridge, I must own I should be wholly surprised, and at a loss, and should infallibly expect the accomplishment of all the rest.

# BAUCIS AND PHILEMON.

### *Imitated from the Eighth Book of Ovid.*

In ancient times, as story tells, The saints would often leave their cells, And stroll about, but hide their quality, To try good people's hospitality.

It happened on a winter night, As authors of the legend write, Two brother hermits, saints by trade, Taking their tour in masquerade, Disguised in tattered habits, went To a small village down in Kent; Where, in the strollers' canting strain, They begged from door to door in vain; Tried every tone might pity win, But not a soul would let them in.

Our wandering saints in woeful state, Treated at this ungodly rate, Having through all the village passed, To a small cottage came at last, Where dwelt a good honest old yeoman, Called, in the neighbourhood, Philemon, Who kindly did these saints invite In his poor hut to pass the night; And then the hospitable Sire Bid goody Baucis mend the fire; While he from out the chimney took A flitch of bacon off the hook, And freely from the fattest side Cut out large slices to be fried; Then stepped aside to fetch 'em drink, Filled a large jug up to the brink, And saw it fairly twice go round; Yet (what is wonderful) they found 'Twas still replenished to the top, As if they ne'er had touched a drop The good old couple were amazed, And often on each other gazed; For both were frightened to the heart, And just began to cry,--What art! Then softly turned aside to view, Whether the lights were burning blue. The gentle pilgrims soon aware on't, Told 'em their calling, and their errant; "Good folks, you need not be afraid, We are but saints," the hermits said; "No hurt shall come to you or yours; But, for that pack of churlish boors, Not fit to live on Christian ground, They and their houses shall be drowned; Whilst you shall see your cottage rise, And grow a church before your eyes."

They scarce had spoke; when fair and soft, The roof began to mount aloft; Aloft rose every beam and rafter, The heavy wall climbed slowly after.

The chimney widened, and grew higher, Became a steeple with a spire.

The kettle to the top was hoist, And there stood fastened to a joist; But with the upside down, to show Its inclination for below. In vain; for a superior force Applied at bottom, stops its coarse, Doomed ever in suspense to dwell, 'Tis now no kettle, but a bell.

A wooden jack, which had almost Lost, by disuse, the art to roast, A sudden alteration feels, Increased by new intestine wheels; And what exalts the wonder more, The number made the motion slower. The flyer, though 't had leaden feet, Turned round so quick, you scarce could see 't; But slackened by some secret power, Now hardly moves an inch an hour. The jack and chimney near allied, Had never left each other's side; The chimney to a steeple grown, The jack would not be left alone; But up against the steeple reared, Became a clock, and still adhered; And still its love to household cares By a shrill voice at noon declares, Warning the cook-maid not to burn That roast meat which it cannot turn.

The groaning chair began to crawl, Like a huge snail along the wall; There stuck aloft in public view; And with small change a pulpit grew.

The porringers, that in a row Hung high, and made a glittering show, To a less noble substance changed, Were now but leathern buckets ranged.

The ballads pasted on the wall, Of Joan of France, and English Moll, Fair Rosamond, and Robin Hood, The Little Children in the Wood, Now seemed to look abundance better, Improved in picture, size, and letter; And high in order placed, describe The heraldry of every tribe.

A bedstead of the antique mode, Compact of timber, many a load, Such as our ancestors did use, Was metamorphosed into pews: Which still their ancient nature keep, By lodging folks disposed to sleep.

The cottage, by such feats as these, Grown to a church by just degrees, The hermits then desired their host To ask for what he fancied most. Philemon having paused a while, Returned 'em thanks in homely style; Then said, "My house is grown so fine, Methinks I still would call it mine: I'm old, and fain would live at ease, Make me the Parson, if you please."

He spoke, and presently he feels His grazier's coat fall down his heels; He sees, yet hardly can believe, About each arm a pudding sleeve; His waistcoat to a cassock grew, And both assumed a sable hue; But being old, continued just As thread-bare, and as full of dust. His talk was now of tithes and dues; He smoked his pipe and read the news; Knew how to preach old sermons next, Vamped in the preface and the text; At christenings well could act his part, And had the service all by heart; Wished women might have children fast, And thought whose sow had farrowed last Against Dissenters would repine, And stood up firm for Right divine. Found his head filled with many a system, But classic authors,--he ne'er missed 'em.

Thus having furbished up a parson, Dame Baucis next they played their farce on. Instead of home-spun coifs were seen Good pinners edg'd with colberteen; Her petticoat transformed apace, Became black satin flounced with lace. Plain Goody would no longer down, 'Twas Madam, in her grogram gown. Philemon was in great surprise, And hardly could believe his eyes, Amazed to see her look so prim; And she admired as much at him.

Thus, happy in their change of life, Were several years this man and wife; When on a day, which proved their last, Discoursing o'er old stories past, They went by chance amidst their talk, To the church yard to take a walk; When Baucis hastily cried out, "My dear, I see your forehead sprout!" "Sprout," quoth the man, "what's this you tell us? I hope you don't believe me jealous, But yet, methinks, I feel it true; And really, yours is budding too-- Nay,--now I cannot stir my foot; It feels as if 'twere taking root."

Description would but tire my Muse; In short, they both were turned to Yews.

Old Goodman Dobson of the green Remembers he the trees has seen; He'll talk of them from noon till night, And goes with folks to show the sight; On Sundays, after evening prayer, He gathers all the parish there, Points out the place of either

Yew: Here Baucis, there Philemon grew, Till once a parson of our town, To mend his barn, cut Baucis down; At which, 'tis hard to be believed How much the other tree was grieved, Grow scrubby, died a-top, was stunted: So the next parson stubbed and burnt it.

# THE LOGICIANS REFUTED.

Logicians have but ill defined As rational, the human kind; Reason, they say, belongs to man, But let them prove it, if they can. Wise Aristotle and Smiglesius, By ratiocinations specious, Have strove to prove with great precision, With definition and division, ***Homo est ratione praeditum***; But, for my soul, I cannot credit 'em. And must, in spite of them, maintain That man and all his ways are vain; And that this boasted lord of nature Is both a weak and erring creature. That instinct is a surer guide Than reason-boasting mortals pride; And, that brute beasts are far before 'em, ***Deus est anima brutorum***. Whoever knew an honest brute, At law his neighbour prosecute, Bring action for assault and battery, Or friend beguile with lies and flattery? O'er plains they ramble unconfined, No politics disturb their mind; They eat their meals, and take their sport, Nor know who's in or out at court. They never to the levee go To treat as dearest friend a foe; They never importune his grace, Nor ever cringe to men in place; Nor undertake a dirty job, Nor draw the quill to write for Bob. Fraught with invective they ne'er go To folks at Paternoster Row: No judges, fiddlers, dancing-masters, No pickpockets, or poetasters Are known to honest quadrupeds: No single brute his fellows leads. Brutes never meet in bloody fray, Nor cut each others' throats for pay. Of beasts, it is confessed, the ape Comes nearest us in human shape; Like man, he imitates each fashion, And malice is his ruling passion: But, both in malice and grimaces, A courtier any ape surpasses. Behold him humbly cringing wait Upon the minister of state; View him, soon after, to inferiors Aping the conduct of superiors: He promises, with equal air, And to perform takes equal care. He, in his turn, finds imitators, At court the porters, lacqueys, waiters Their masters' manners still contract, And footmen, lords, and dukes can act. Thus, at the court, both great and small Behave alike, for all ape all.

# THE PUPPET SHOW.

The life of man to represent,
  And turn it all to ridicule,
Wit did a puppet-show invent,
  Where the chief actor is a fool.

The gods of old were logs of wood,
  And worship was to puppets paid;
In antic dress the idol stood,
  And priests and people bowed the head.

No wonder then, if art began
  The simple votaries to frame,
To shape in timber foolish man,
  And consecrate the block to fame.

From hence poetic fancy learned
  That trees might rise from human forms
The body to a trunk be turned,
  And branches issue from the arms.

Thus Daedalus and Ovid too,
  That man's a blockhead have confessed,
Powel and Stretch {1} the hint pursue;
  Life is the farce, the world a jest.

The same great truth South Sea hath proved
  On that famed theatre, the ally,
Where thousands by directors moved
  Are now sad monuments of folly.

What Momus was of old to Jove
  The same harlequin is now;
The former was buffoon above,
  The latter is a Punch below.

This fleeting scene is but a stage,
  Where various images appear,
In different parts of youth and age
  Alike the prince and peasant share.

Some draw our eyes by being great,
  False pomp conceals mere wood within,
And legislators rang'd in state
  Are oft but wisdom in machine.

A stock may chance to wear a crown,
  And timber as a lord take place,
A statue may put on a frown,
  And cheat us with a thinking face.

Others are blindly led away,
  And made to act for ends unknown,
By the mere spring of wires they play,
  And speak in language not their own.

Too oft, alas! a scolding wife
  Usurps a jolly fellow's throne,
And many drink the cup of life
  Mix'd and embittered by a Joan.

In short, whatever men pursue
  Of pleasure, folly, war, or love,

This mimic-race brings all to view,
  Alike they dress, they talk, they move.

Go on, great Stretch, with artful hand,
  Mortals to please and to deride,
And when death breaks thy vital band
  Thou shalt put on a puppet's pride.

Thou shalt in puny wood be shown,
  Thy image shall preserve thy fame,
Ages to come thy worth shall own,
  Point at thy limbs, and tell thy name.

Tell Tom he draws a farce in vain,
  Before he looks in nature's glass;
Puns cannot form a witty scene,
  Nor pedantry for humour pass.

To make men act as senseless wood,
  And chatter in a mystic strain,
Is a mere force on flesh and blood,
  And shows some error in the brain.

He that would thus refine on thee,
  And turn thy stage into a school,
The jest of Punch will ever be,
  And stand confessed the greater fool.

# CADENUS AND VANESSA.

*Written Anno 1713.*

The shepherds and the nymphs were seen Pleading before the Cyprian Queen. The counsel for the fair began Accusing the false creature, man.

The brief with weighty crimes was charged, On which the pleader much enlarged: That Cupid now has lost his art, Or blunts the point of every dart; His altar now no longer smokes; His mother's aid no youth invokes-- This tempts free-thinkers to refine, And bring in doubt their powers divine, Now love is dwindled to intrigue, And marriage grown a money-league. Which crimes aforesaid (with her leave) Were (as he humbly did conceive) Against our Sovereign Lady's peace, Against the statutes in that case, Against her dignity and crown: Then prayed an answer and sat down.

The nymphs with scorn beheld their foes: When the defendant's counsel rose, And, what no lawyer ever lacked, With impudence owned all the fact. But, what the gentlest heart would vex, Laid all the fault on t'other sex. That modern love is no such thing As what those ancient poets sing; A fire celestial, chaste, refined, Conceived and kindled in the mind, Which having found an equal flame, Unites, and both become the same, In different breasts together burn, Together both to ashes turn. But women now feel no such fire, And only know the gross desire; Their passions move in lower spheres, Where'er caprice or folly steers. A dog, a parrot, or an ape, Or some worse brute in human shape Engross the fancies of the fair, The few soft moments they can spare From visits to receive and pay, From scandal, politics, and play, From fans, and flounces, and brocades, From equipage and park-parades, From all the thousand female toys, From every trifle that employs The out or inside of their heads Between their toilets and their beds.

In a dull stream, which, moving slow, You hardly see the current flow, If a small breeze obstructs the course, It whirls about for want of force, And in its narrow circle gathers Nothing but chaff, and straws, and feathers: The current of a female mind Stops thus, and turns with every wind; Thus whirling round, together draws Fools, fops, and rakes, for chaff and straws. Hence we conclude, no women's hearts Are won by virtue, wit, and parts; Nor are the men of sense to blame For breasts incapable of flame: The fault must on the nymphs be placed, Grown so corrupted in their taste.

The pleader having spoke his best, Had witness ready to attest, Who fairly could on oath depose, When questions on the fact arose, That every article was true; *Nor further those deponents knew*: Therefore he humbly would insist, The bill might be with costs dismissed.

The cause appeared of so much weight, That Venus from the judgment-seat Desired them not to talk so loud, Else she must interpose a cloud: For if the heavenly folk should know These pleadings in the Courts below, That mortals here disdain to love, She ne'er could show her face above. For gods, their betters, are too wise To value that which men despise. "And then," said she, "my son and I Must stroll in air 'twixt earth and sky: Or else, shut out from heaven and earth, Fly to the sea, my place of birth; There live with daggled mermaids pent, And keep on fish perpetual Lent."

But since the case appeared so nice, She thought it best to take advice. The Muses, by their king's permission, Though foes to love, attend the session, And on the right hand took their places In order; on the left, the Graces: To whom she might her doubts propose On all emergencies that rose. The Muses oft were seen to frown; The Graces half ashamed look down; And 'twas observed, there were but few Of either sex, among the crew, Whom she or her assessors knew. The goddess soon began to see Things were not ripe for a decree, And said she must consult her books, The lovers' Fletas, Bractons, Cokes. First to a dapper clerk she beckoned, To turn to Ovid, book the second; She then referred them to a place In Virgil (*vide* Dido's case); As for Tibullus's reports, They never passed for law in Courts: For Cowley's brief, and pleas of Waller, Still their authority is smaller.

There was on both sides much to say; She'd hear the cause another day; And so she did, and then a third, She heard it--there she kept her word; But with rejoinders and replies, Long bills, and answers, stuffed with lies Demur, imparlance, and essoign, The parties ne'er could issue join: For sixteen years the cause was spun, And then stood where it first begun.

Now, gentle Clio, sing or say, What Venus meant by this delay. The goddess, much perplexed in mind, To see her empire thus declined, When first this grand debate arose Above her wisdom to compose, Conceived a project in her head, To work her ends; which, if it sped, Would show the merits of the cause Far better than consulting laws.

In a glad hour Lucina's aid Produced on earth a wondrous maid, On whom the queen of love was bent To try a new experiment. She threw her law-books on the shelf, And thus debated with herself:--

"Since men allege they ne'er can find Those beauties in a female mind Which raise a flame that will endure For ever, uncorrupt and pure; If 'tis with reason they complain, This infant shall restore my reign. I'll search where every virtue dwells, From Courts inclusive down to cells. What preachers talk, or sages write, These I will gather and unite, And represent them to mankind Collected in that infant's mind."

This said, she plucks in heaven's high bowers A sprig of Amaranthine flowers, In nectar thrice infuses bays, Three times refined in Titan's rays: Then calls the Graces to her aid, And sprinkles thrice the now-born maid. From whence the tender skin assumes A sweetness above all perfumes; From whence a cleanliness remains, Incapable of outward stains; From whence that decency of mind, So lovely in a female kind. Where not one careless thought intrudes Less modest than the speech of prudes; Where never blush was called in aid, The spurious virtue in a maid, A virtue but at second-hand; They blush because they understand.

The Graces next would act their part, And show but little of their art; Their work was half already done, The child with native beauty shone, The outward form no help required: Each breathing on her thrice, inspired That gentle, soft, engaging air Which in old times adorned the fair, And said, "Vanessa be the name By which thou shalt be known to fame; Vanessa, by the gods enrolled: Her name on earth-- shall not be told."

But still the work was not complete, When Venus thought on a deceit: Drawn by her doves, away she flies, And finds out Pallas in the skies: Dear Pallas, I have been this morn To see a lovely infant born: A boy in yonder isle below, So like my own without his bow, By beauty could your heart be won, You'd swear it is Apollo's son; But it shall ne'er be said, a child So hopeful has by me been spoiled; I have enough besides to spare, And give him wholly to your care.

Wisdom's above suspecting wiles; The queen of learning gravely smiles, Down from Olympus comes with joy, Mistakes Vanessa for a boy; Then sows within her tender mind Seeds long unknown to womankind; For manly bosoms chiefly fit, The seeds of knowledge, judgment, wit, Her soul was suddenly endued With justice, truth, and fortitude; With honour, which no breath can stain, Which malice must attack in vain: With open heart and bounteous hand: But Pallas here was at a stand; She know in our degenerate days Bare virtue could not live on praise, That meat must be with money bought: She therefore, upon second thought, Infused yet as it were by stealth, Some small regard for state and wealth: Of which as she grew up there stayed A tincture in the prudent maid: She managed her estate with care, Yet liked three footmen to her chair, But lest he should neglect his studies Like a young heir, the thrifty goddess (For fear young master should be spoiled) Would use him like a younger child; And, after long computing, found 'Twould come to just five thousand pound.

The Queen of Love was pleased and proud To we Vanessa thus endowed; She doubted not but such a dame Through every breast would dart a flame; That every rich and lordly swain With pride would drag about her chain; That scholars would forsake their books To study bright Vanessa's looks: As she advanced that woman-kind Would by her model form their mind, And all their conduct would be tried By her, as an unerring guide. Offending daughters oft would hear Vanessa's praise rung in their ear: Miss Betty, when she does a fault, Lets fall her knife, or spills the salt, Will thus be by her mother chid, "'Tis what Vanessa never did." Thus by the nymphs and swains adored, My power shall be again restored, And happy lovers bless my reign-- So Venus hoped, but hoped in vain.

For when in time the martial maid Found out the trick that Venus played, She shakes her helm, she knits her brows, And fired with indignation, vows To-morrow, ere the setting sun, She'd all undo that she had done.

But in the poets we may find A wholesome law, time out of mind, Had been confirmed by Fate's decree; That gods, of whatso'er degree, Resume not what themselves have given, Or any brother-god in Heaven; Which keeps the peace among the gods, Or they must always be at odds. And Pallas, if she broke the laws, Must yield her foe the stronger cause; A shame to one so much adored For Wisdom, at Jove's council-board. Besides, she feared the queen of love Would meet with better friends above. And though she must with grief reflect To see a mortal virgin deck'd

With graces hitherto unknown To female breasts, except her own, Yet she would act as best became A goddess of unspotted fame; She knew, by augury divine, Venus would fail in her design: She studied well the point, and found Her foe's conclusions were not sound, From premises erroneous brought, And therefore the deduction's nought, And must have contrary effects To what her treacherous foe expects.

In proper season Pallas meets The queen of love, whom thus she greets (For Gods, we are by Homer told, Can in celestial language scold), "Perfidious Goddess! but in vain You formed this project in your brain, A project for thy talents fit, With much deceit, and little wit; Thou hast, as thou shalt quickly see, Deceived thyself instead of me; For how can heavenly wisdom prove An instrument to earthly love? Know'st thou not yet that men commence Thy votaries, for want of sense? Nor shall Vanessa be the theme To manage thy abortive scheme; She'll prove the greatest of thy foes, And yet I scorn to interpose, But using neither skill nor force, Leave all things to their natural course."

The goddess thus pronounced her doom, When, lo, Vanessa in her bloom, Advanced like Atalanta's star, But rarely seen, and seen from far: In a new world with caution stepped, Watched all the company she kept, Well knowing from the books she read What dangerous paths young virgins tread; Would seldom at the park appear, Nor saw the play-house twice a year; Yet not incurious, was inclined To know the converse of mankind.

First issued from perfumers' shops A crowd of fashionable fops; They liked her how she liked the play? Then told the tattle of the day, A duel fought last night at two About a lady--you know who; Mentioned a new Italian, come Either from Muscovy or Rome; Gave hints of who and who's together; Then fell to talking of the weather: Last night was so extremely fine, The ladies walked till after nine. Then in soft voice, and speech absurd, With nonsense every second word, With fustian from exploded plays, They celebrate her beauty's praise, Run o'er their cant of stupid lies, And tell the murders of her eyes.

With silent scorn Vanessa sat, Scarce list'ning to their idle chat; Further than sometimes by a frown, When they grew pert, to pull them down. At last she spitefully was bent To try their wisdom's full extent; And said, she valued nothing less Than titles, figure, shape, and dress; That merit should be chiefly placed In judgment, knowledge, wit, and taste; And these, she offered to dispute, Alone distinguished man from brute: That present times have no pretence To virtue, in the noble sense By Greeks and Romans understood, To perish for our country's good. She named the ancient heroes round, Explained for what they were renowned; Then spoke with censure, or applause, Of foreign customs, rites, and laws; Through nature and through art she ranged, And gracefully her subject changed: In vain; her hearers had no share In all she spoke, except to stare. Their judgment was upon the whole, --That lady is the dullest soul-- Then tipped their forehead in a jeer, As who should say--she wants it here; She may be handsome, young, and rich, But none will burn her for a witch.

A party next of glittering dames, From round the purlieus of St. James, Came early, out of pure goodwill, To see the girl in deshabille. Their clamour 'lighting from their chairs, Grew louder, all the way up stairs; At entrance loudest, where they found The room with volumes littered round, Vanessa held Montaigne, and read, Whilst Mrs. Susan combed her head: They called for tea and chocolate, And fell into their usual chat, Discoursing with important face, On ribbons, fans, and gloves, and lace: Showed patterns just from India brought, And gravely asked her what she thought, Whether the red or green were best, And what they cost? Vanessa guessed, As came into her fancy first, Named half the rates, and liked the worst. To scandal next--What awkward thing Was that, last Sunday, in the ring? I'm sorry Mopsa breaks so fast; I said her face would never last, Corinna with that youthful air, Is thirty, and a bit to spare. Her fondness for a certain earl Began, when I was but a girl. Phyllis, who but a month ago Was married to the Tunbridge beau, I saw coquetting t'other night In public with that odious knight.

They rallied next Vanessa's dress; That gown was made for old Queen Bess. Dear madam, let me set your head; Don't you intend to put on red? A petticoat without a hoop! Sure, you are not ashamed to stoop; With handsome garters at your knees, No matter what a fellow sees.

Filled with disdain, with rage inflamed, Both of herself and sex ashamed, The nymph stood silent out of spite, Nor would vouchsafe to set them right. Away the fair detractors went, And gave, by turns, their censures vent. She's not so handsome in my eyes: For wit, I wonder where it lies. She's fair and clean, and that's the most; But why proclaim her for a toast? A baby face, no life, no airs, But what she learnt at country fairs. Scarce knows what difference is between Rich Flanders lace, and

Colberteen. I'll undertake my little Nancy, In flounces has a better fancy. With all her wit, I would not ask Her judgment, how to buy a mask. We begged her but to patch her face, She never hit one proper place; Which every girl at five years old Can do as soon as she is told. I own, that out-of-fashion stuff Becomes the creature well enough. The girl might pass, if we could get her To know the world a little better. ( *To know the world*! a modern phrase For visits, ombre, balls, and plays.)

Thus, to the world's perpetual shame, The queen of beauty lost her aim, Too late with grief she understood Pallas had done more harm than good; For great examples are but vain, Where ignorance begets disdain. Both sexes, armed with guilt and spite, Against Vanessa's power unite; To copy her few nymphs aspired; Her virtues fewer swains admired; So stars, beyond a certain height, Give mortals neither heat nor light.

Yet some of either sex, endowed With gifts superior to the crowd, With virtue, knowledge, taste, and wit, She condescended to admit; With pleasing arts she could reduce Men's talents to their proper use; And with address each genius hold To that wherein it most excelled; Thus making others' wisdom known, Could please them and improve her own. A modest youth said something new, She placed it in the strongest view. All humble worth she strove to raise; Would not be praised, yet loved to praise. The learned met with free approach, Although they came not in a coach. Some clergy too she would allow, Nor quarreled at their awkward bow. But this was for Cadenus' sake; A gownman of a different make. Whom Pallas, once Vanessa's tutor, Had fixed on for her coadjutor.

But Cupid, full of mischief, longs To vindicate his mother's wrongs. On Pallas all attempts are vain; One way he knows to give her pain; Vows on Vanessa's heart to take Due vengeance, for her patron's sake. Those early seeds by Venus sown, In spite of Pallas, now were grown; And Cupid hoped they would improve By time, and ripen into love. The boy made use of all his craft, In vain discharging many a shaft, Pointed at colonels, lords, and beaux; Cadenus warded off the blows, For placing still some book betwixt, The darts were in the cover fixed, Or often blunted and recoiled, On Plutarch's morals struck, were spoiled.

The queen of wisdom could foresee, But not prevent the Fates decree; And human caution tries in vain To break that adamantine chain. Vanessa, though by Pallas taught, By love invulnerable thought, Searching in books for wisdom's aid,

Was, in the very search, betrayed.

Cupid, though all his darts were lost, Yet still resolved to spare no cost; He could not answer to his fame The triumphs of that stubborn dame, A nymph so hard to be subdued, Who neither was coquette nor prude. I find, says he, she wants a doctor, Both to adore her, and instruct her: I'll give her what she most admires, Among those venerable sires. Cadenus is a subject fit, Grown old in politics and wit; Caressed by Ministers of State, Of half mankind the dread and hate. Whate'er vexations love attend, She need no rivals apprehend Her sex, with universal voice, Must laugh at her capricious choice.

Cadenus many things had writ, Vanessa much esteemed his wit, And called for his poetic works! Meantime the boy in secret lurks. And while the book was in her hand, The urchin from his private stand Took aim, and shot with all his strength A dart of such prodigious length, It pierced the feeble volume through, And deep transfixed her bosom too. Some lines, more moving than the rest, Struck to the point that pierced her breast; And, borne directly to the heart, With pains unknown, increased her smart.

Vanessa, not in years a score, Dreams of a gown of forty-four; Imaginary charms can find, In eyes with reading almost blind; Cadenus now no more appears Declined in health, advanced in years. She fancies music in his tongue, Nor farther looks, but thinks him young. What mariner is not afraid To venture in a ship decayed? What planter will attempt to yoke A sapling with a falling oak? As years increase, she brighter shines, Cadenus with each day declines, And he must fall a prey to Time, While she continues in her prime.

Cadenus, common forms apart, In every scene had kept his heart; Had sighed and languished, vowed and writ, For pastime, or to show his wit; But time, and books, and State affairs, Had spoiled his fashionable airs, He now could praise, esteem, approve, But understood not what was love. His conduct might have made him styled A father, and the nymph his child. That innocent delight he took To see the virgin mind her book, Was but the master's secret joy In school to hear the finest boy. Her knowledge with her fancy grew, She hourly pressed for something new; Ideas came into her mind So fact, his lessons lagged behind; She reasoned, without plodding long, Nor ever gave her judgment wrong. But now a sudden change was wrought, She minds no longer what he taught. Cadenus was amazed to find Such marks of a distracted mind; For though she seemed to listen more To all he spoke, than e'er before. He found her thoughts would absent range, Yet guessed not whence could spring the change. And first he modestly conjectures, His pupil might be tired with lectures, Which helped to mortify his pride, Yet gave him not the heart to chide; But in a mild dejected strain, At last he ventured to complain: Said, she should be no longer teased, Might have her freedom when she pleased; Was now convinced he acted wrong, To hide her from the world so long, And in dull studies to engage One of her tender sex and age. That every nymph with envy owned, How she might shine in the *Grande-Monde*, And every shepherd was undone, To see her cloistered like a nun. This was a visionary scheme, He waked, and found it but a dream; A project far above his skill, For Nature must be Nature still. If she was bolder than became A scholar to a courtly dame, She might excuse a man of letters; Thus tutors often treat their betters, And since his talk offensive grew, He came to take his last adieu.

Vanessa, filled with just disdain, Would still her dignity maintain, Instructed from her early years To scorn the art of female tears.

Had he employed his time so long, To teach her what was right or wrong, Yet could such notions entertain, That all his lectures were in vain? She owned the wand'ring of her thoughts, But he must answer for her faults. She well remembered, to her cost, That all his lessons were not lost. Two maxims she could still produce, And sad experience taught her use; That virtue, pleased by being shown, Knows nothing which it dare not own; Can make us without fear disclose Our inmost secrets to our foes; That common forms were not designed Directors to a noble mind. Now, said the nymph, I'll let you see My actions with your rules agree, That I can vulgar forms despise, And have no secrets to disguise. I knew by what you said and writ, How dangerous things were men of wit; You cautioned me against their charms, But never gave me equal arms; Your lessons found the weakest part, Aimed at the head, but reached the heart.

Cadenus felt within him rise Shame, disappointment, guilt, surprise. He know not how to reconcile Such language, with her usual style: And yet her words were so expressed, He could not hope she spoke in jest. His thoughts had wholly been confined To form and cultivate her mind. He hardly knew, till he was told, Whether the nymph were young or old; Had met her in a public place, Without distinguishing her face, Much less could his declining age Vanessa's earliest thoughts engage. And if her youth indifference met, His person must contempt beget, Or grant her passion be sincere, How shall his innocence be clear? Appearances were all so strong, The world must think him in the wrong; Would say he made a treach'rous use. Of wit, to flatter and seduce; The town would swear he had betrayed, By magic spells, the harmless maid; And every beau would have his jokes, That scholars were like other folks; That when Platonic flights were over, The tutor turned a mortal lover. So tender of the young and fair; It showed a true paternal care-- Five thousand guineas in her purse; The doctor might have fancied worst,-- Hardly at length he silence broke, And faltered every word he spoke; Interpreting her complaisance, Just as a man sans consequence. She rallied well, he always knew; Her manner now was something new; And what she spoke was in an air, As serious as a tragic player. But those who aim at ridicule, Should fix upon some certain rule, Which fairly hints they are in jest, Else he must enter his protest; For let a man be ne'er so wise, He may be caught with sober lies; A science which he never taught, And, to be free, was dearly bought; For, take it in its proper light, 'Tis just what coxcombs call a bite.

But not to dwell on things minute, Vanessa finished the dispute, Brought weighty arguments to prove, That reason was her guide in love. She thought he had himself described, His doctrines when she fist imbibed; What he had planted now was grown, His virtues she might call her own; As he approves, as he dislikes, Love or contempt her fancy strikes. Self-love in nature rooted fast, Attends us first, and leaves us last: Why she likes him, admire not at her, She loves herself, and that's the matter. How was her tutor wont to praise The geniuses of ancient days! (Those authors he so oft had named For learning, wit, and wisdom famed). Was struck with love, esteem, and awe, For persons whom he never saw. Suppose Cadenus flourished then, He must adore such God-like men. If one short volume could comprise All that was witty, learned, and wise, How would it be esteemed, and read, Although the writer long were dead? If such an author were alive, How all would for his friendship strive; And come in crowds to see his face? And this she takes to be her case. Cadenus answers every end, The book, the author, and the friend, The utmost her desires will reach, Is but to learn what he can teach; His converse is a system fit Alone to fill up all her wit; While ev'ry passion of her mind In him is centred and confined.

Love can with speech inspire a mute, And taught Vanessa to dispute. This topic, never touched before, Displayed her eloquence the more: Her knowledge, with such pains acquired, By this new passion grew inspired. Through this she made all objects pass, Which gave a tincture o'er the mass; As rivers, though they bend and twine, Still to the sea their course incline; Or, as philosophers, who find Some fav'rite system to their mind, In every point to make it fit, Will force all nature to submit.

Cadenus, who could ne'er suspect His lessons would have such effect, Or be so artfully applied, Insensibly came on her side; It was an unforeseen event, Things took a turn he never meant. Whoe'er excels in what we prize, Appears a hero to our eyes; Each girl, when pleased with what is taught, Will have the teacher in her thought. When miss delights in her spinnet, A fiddler may a fortune get; A blockhead, with melodious voice In boarding-schools can have his choice; And oft the dancing-master's art Climbs from the toe to touch the heart. In learning let a nymph delight, The pedant gets a mistress by't. Cadenus, to his grief and shame, Could scarce oppose Vanessa's flame; But though her arguments were strong, At least could hardly with them wrong. Howe'er it came, he could not tell, But, sure, she never talked so well. His pride began to interpose, Preferred before a crowd of beaux, So bright a nymph to come unsought, Such wonder by his merit wrought; 'Tis merit must with her prevail, He never know her judgment fail. She noted all she ever read, And had a most discerning head.

'Tis an old maxim in the schools, That vanity's the food of fools; Yet now and then your men of wit Will condescend to take a bit.

So when Cadenus could not hide, He chose to justify his pride; Construing the passion she had shown, Much to her praise, more to his own. Nature in him had merit placed, In her, a most judicious taste. Love, hitherto a transient guest, Ne'er held possession in his breast; So long attending at the gate, Disdain'd to enter in so late. Love, why do we one passion call? When 'tis a compound of them all; Where hot and cold, where sharp and sweet, In all their equipages meet; Where pleasures mixed with pains appear, Sorrow with joy, and hope with fear. Wherein his dignity and age Forbid Cadenus to engage. But friendship in its greatest height, A constant, rational delight, On virtue's basis fixed to last, When love's allurements long are past; Which gently warms, but cannot burn; He gladly offers in return; His want of passion will redeem, With gratitude, respect, esteem; With that devotion we bestow, When goddesses appear below.

While thus Cadenus entertains Vanessa in exalted strains, The nymph in sober words intreats A truce with all sublime conceits. For why such raptures, flights, and fancies, To her who durst not read romances; In lofty style to make replies, Which he had taught her to despise? But when her tutor will affect Devotion, duty, and respect, He fairly abdicates his throne, The government is now her own; He has a forfeiture incurred, She vows to take him at his word, And hopes he will not take it strange If both should now their stations change The nymph will have her turn, to be The tutor; and the pupil he: Though she already can discern Her scholar is not apt to learn; Or wants capacity to reach The science she designs to teach; Wherein his genius was below The skill of every common beau; Who, though he cannot spell, is wise Enough to read a lady's eyes? And will each accidental glance Interpret for a kind advance.

But what success Vanessa met Is to the world a secret yet; Whether the nymph, to please her swain, Talks in a high romantic strain; Or whether he at last descends To like with less seraphic ends; Or to compound the bus'ness, whether They temper love and books together; Must never to mankind be told, Nor shall the conscious muse unfold.

Meantime the mournful queen of love Led but a weary life above. She ventures now to leave the skies, Grown by Vanessa's conduct wise. For though by one perverse event Pallas had crossed her first intent, Though her design was not obtained, Yet had she much experience gained; And, by the project vainly tried, Could better now the cause decide. She gave due notice that both parties, *Coram Regina prox' die Martis*, Should at their peril without fail Come and appear, and save their bail. All met, and silence thrice proclaimed, One lawyer to each side was named. The judge discovered in her face Resentments for her late disgrace; And, full of anger, shame, and grief, Directed them to mind their brief; Nor spend their time to show their reading, She'd have a summary proceeding. She gathered under every head, The sum of what each lawyer said; Gave her own reasons last; and then Decreed the cause against the men.

But, in a weighty case like this, To show she did not judge amiss, Which evil tongues might else report, She made a speech in open court; Wherein she grievously complains, "How she was cheated by the swains." On whose petition (humbly showing That women were not worth the wooing, And that unless the sex would mend, The race of lovers soon must end); "She was at Lord knows what expense, To form a nymph of wit and sense; A model for her sex designed, Who never could one lover find, She saw her favour was misplaced; The follows had a wretched taste; She needs must tell them to their face, They were a senseless, stupid race; And were she to begin again, She'd study to reform the men; Or add some grains of folly more To women than they had before. To put them on an equal foot; And this, or nothing else, would do't. This might their mutual fancy strike, Since every being loves its like.

But now, repenting what was done, She left all business to her son; She puts the world in his possession, And let him use it at discretion."

The crier was ordered to dismiss The court, so made his last O yes! The goddess would no longer wait, But rising from her chair of state, Left all below at six and seven, Harnessed her doves, and flew to Heaven.

# STELLA'S BIRTHDAY, 1718.

Stella this day is thirty-four (We shan't dispute a year or more) However, Stella, be not troubled, Although thy size and years are doubled Since first I saw thee at sixteen, The brightest virgin on the green. So little is thy form declined; Made up so largely in thy mind.

Oh, would it please the gods to split Thy beauty, size, and years, and wit, No age could furnish out a pair Of nymphs so graceful, wise, and fair: With half the lustre of your eyes, With half your wit, your years, and size. And then, before it grew too late, How should I beg of gentle fate, (That either nymph might lack her swain), To split my worship too in twain.

# STELLA'S BIRTHDAY, 1720.

All travellers at first incline Where'er they see the fairest sign; And if they find the chambers neat, And like the liquor and the meat, Will call again and recommend The Angel Inn to every friend What though the painting grows decayed, The house will never lose its trade: Nay, though the treach'rous tapster Thomas Hangs a new angel two doors from us, As fine as daubers' hands can make it, In hopes that strangers may mistake it, We think it both a shame and sin, To quit the true old Angel Inn.

Now, this is Stella's case in fact, An angel's face, a little cracked (Could poets, or could painters fix How angels look at, thirty-six): This drew us in at first, to find In such a form an angel's mind; And every virtue now supplies The fainting rays of Stella's eyes. See, at her levee, crowding swains, Whom Stella freely entertains, With breeding, humour, wit, and sense; And puts them but to small expense; Their mind so plentifully fills, And makes such reasonable bills, So little gets for what she gives, We really wonder how she lives! And had her stock been less, no doubt, She must have long ago run out.

Then who can think we'll quit the place, When Doll hangs out a newer face; Or stop and light at Cloe's Head, With scraps and leavings to be fed.

Then Cloe, still go on to prate Of thirty-six, and thirty-eight; Pursue your trade of scandal picking, Your hints that Stella is no chicken. Your innuendoes when you tell us, That Stella loves to talk with fellows; And let me warn you to believe A truth, for which your soul should grieve: That should you live to see the day When Stella's locks, must all be grey, When age must print a furrowed trace On every feature of her face; Though you and all your senseless tribe, Could art, or time, or nature bribe To make you look like beauty's queen, And hold for ever at fifteen; No bloom of youth can ever blind The cracks and wrinkles of your mind; All men of sense will pass your door, And crowd to Stella's at fourscore.

# STELLA'S BIRTHDAY.

***A great bottle of wine, long buried, being that day dug up. 1722.***

Resolved my annual verse to pay, By duty bound, on Stella's day; Furnished with paper, pens, and ink, I gravely sat me down to think: I bit my nails, and scratched my head, But found my wit and fancy fled; Or, if with more than usual pain, A thought came slowly from my brain, It cost me Lord knows how much time To shape it into sense and rhyme; And, what was yet a greater curse, Long-thinking made my fancy worse

Forsaken by th' inspiring nine, I waited at Apollo's shrine; I told him what the world would sa If Stella were unsung to-day; How I should hide my head for shame, When both the Jacks and Robin came; How Ford would frown, how Jim would leer, How Sh---r the rogue would sneer, And swear it does not always follow, That ***Semel'n anno ridet*** Apollo. I have assured them twenty times, That Phoebus helped me in my rhymes, Phoebus inspired me from above, And he and I were hand and glove. But finding me so dull and dry since, They'll call it all poetic licence. And when I brag of aid divine, Think Eusden's right as good as mine.

Nor do I ask for Stella's sake; 'Tis my own credit lies at stake. And Stella will be sung, while I Can only be a stander by.

Apollo having thought a little, Returned this answer to a tittle.

Tho' you should live like old Methusalem, I furnish hints, and you should use all 'em, You yearly sing as she grows old, You'd leave her virtues half untold. But to say truth, such dulness reigns Through the whole set of Irish Deans; I'm daily stunned with such a medley, Dean W---, Dean D---l, and Dean S---; That let what Dean soever come, My orders are, I'm not at home; And if your voice had not been loud, You must have passed among the crowd.

But, now your danger to prevent, You must apply to Mrs. Brent, {2} For she, as priestess, knows the rites Wherein the God of Earth delights. First, nine ways looking, let her stand With an old poker in her hand; Let her describe a circle round In Saunder's {3} cellar on the ground A spade let prudent Archy {4} hold, And with discretion dig the mould; Let Stella look with watchful eye, Rebecea, Ford, and

Grattons by.

Behold the bottle, where it lies With neck elated tow'rds the skies! The god of winds, and god of fire, Did to its wondrous birth conspire; And Bacchus for the poet's use Poured in a strong inspiring juice: See! as you raise it from its tomb, It drags behind a spacious womb, And in the spacious womb contains A sovereign med'cine for the brains.

You'll find it soon, if fate consents; If not, a thousand Mrs. Brents, Ten thousand Archys arm'd with spades, May dig in vain to Pluto's shades.

From thence a plenteous draught infuse, And boldly then invoke the muse (But first let Robert on his knees With caution drain it from the lees); The muse will at your call appear, With Stella's praise to crown the year.

# STELLA'S BIRTHDAY, 1724.

As when a beauteous nymph decays, We say she's past her dancing days; So poets lose their feet by time, And can no longer dance in rhyme. Your annual bard had rather chose To celebrate your birth in prose; Yet merry folks who want by chance A pair to make a country dance, Call the old housekeeper, and get her To fill a place, for want of better; While Sheridan is off the hooks, And friend Delany at his books, That Stella may avoid disgrace, Once more the Dean supplies their place.

Beauty and wit, too sad a truth, Have always been confined to youth; The god of wit, and beauty's queen, He twenty-one, and she fifteen; No poet ever sweetly sung. Unless he were like Phoebus, young; Nor ever nymph inspired to rhyme, Unless like Venus in her prime. At fifty-six, if this be true, Am I a poet fit for you; Or at the age of forty-three, Are you a subject fit for me? Adieu bright wit, and radiant eyes; You must be grave, and I be wise. Our fate in vain we would oppose, But I'll be still your friend in prose; Esteem and friendship to express, Will not require poetic dress; And if the muse deny her aid To have them sung, they may be said.

But, Stella say, what evil tongue Reports you are no longer young? That Time sits with his scythe to mow Where erst sat Cupid with his bow; That half your locks are turned to grey; I'll ne'er believe a word they say. 'Tis true, but let it not be known, My eyes are somewhat dimish grown; For nature, always in the right, To your decays adapts my sight, And wrinkles undistinguished pass, For I'm ashamed to use a glass; And till I see them with these eyes, Whoever says you have them, lies.

No length of time can make you quit Honour and virtue, sense and wit, Thus you may still be young to me, While I can better hear than see: Oh, ne'er may fortune show her spite, To make me deaf, and mend my sight.

# STELLA'S BIRTHDAY, MARCH 13, 1726.

This day, whate'er the Fates decree, Shall still be kept with joy by me; This day, then, let us not be told That you are sick, and I grown old, Nor think on our approaching ills, And talk of spectacles and pills; To-morrow will be time enough To hear such mortifying stuff. Yet, since from reason may be brought A better and more pleasing thought, Which can, in spite of all decays, Support a few remaining days: From not the gravest of divines Accept for once some serious lines.

Although we now can form no more Long schemes of life, as heretofore; Yet you, while time is running fast, Can look with joy on what is past.

Were future happiness and pain A mere contrivance of the brain, As Atheists argue, to entice, And fit their proselytes for vice (The only comfort they propose, To have companions in their woes). Grant this the case, yet sure 'tis hard That virtue, styled its own reward, And by all sages understood To be the chief of human good, Should acting, die, or leave behind Some lasting pleasure in the mind. Which by remembrance will assuage Grief, sickness, poverty, and age; And strongly shoot a radiant dart, To shine through life's declining part.

Say, Stella, feel you no content, Reflecting on a life well spent; Your skilful hand employed to save Despairing wretches from the grave; And then supporting with your store, Those whom you dragged from death before? So Providence on mortals waits, Preserving what it first creates, You generous boldness to defend An innocent and absent friend; That courage which can make you just, To merit humbled in the dust; The detestation you express For vice in all its glittering dress: That patience under to torturing pain, Where stubborn stoics would complain.

Must these like empty shadows pass, Or forms reflected from a glass? Or mere chimaeras in the mind, That fly, and leave no marks behind? Does not the body thrive and grow By food of twenty years ago? And, had it not been still supplied, It must a thousand times have died. Then, who with reason can maintain That no effects of food remain? And, is not virtue in mankind The nutriment that feeds the mind? Upheld by each good action past, And still continued by the last: Then, who with reason can pretend That all effects of virtue end?

Believe me, Stella, when you show That true contempt for things below, Nor prize your life for other ends Than merely to oblige your friends, Your former actions claim their part, And join to fortify your heart.  For virtue in her daily race, Like Janus, bears a double face. Look back with joy where she has gone, And therefore goes with courage on. She at your sickly couch will wait, And guide you to a better state.

O then, whatever heav'n intends, Take pity on your pitying friends; Nor let your ills affect your mind, To fancy they can be unkind; Me, surely me, you ought to spare, Who gladly would your sufferings share; Or give my scrap of life to you, And think it far beneath your due; You to whose care so oft I owe That I'm alive to tell you so.

# TO STELLA,

### *Visiting me in my sickness*, *October*, 1727.

Pallas, observing Stella's wit Was more than for her sex was fit; And that her beauty, soon or late, Might breed confusion in the state; In high concern for human kind, Fixed honour in her infant mind.

But (not in wranglings to engage With such a stupid vicious age), If honour I would here define, It answers faith in things divine. As natural life the body warms, And, scholars teach, the soul informs; So honour animates the whole, And is the spirit of the soul.

Those numerous virtues which the tribe Of tedious moralists describe, And by such various titles call, True honour comprehends them all. Let melancholy rule supreme, Choler preside, or blood, or phlegm. It makes no difference in the case. Nor is complexion honour's place.

But, lest we should for honour take The drunken quarrels of a rake, Or think it seated in a scar, Or on a proud triumphal car, Or in the payment of a debt, We lose with sharpers at piquet; Or, when a whore in her vocation, Keeps punctual to an assignation; Or that on which his lordship swears, When vulgar knaves would lose their ears: Let Stella's fair example preach A lesson she alone can teach.

In points of honour to be tried, All passions must be laid aside; Ask no advice, but think alone, Suppose the question not your own; How shall I act? is not the case, But how would Brutus in my place; In such a cause would Cato bleed; And how would Socrates proceed?

Drive all objections from your mind, Else you relapse to human kind; Ambition, avarice, and lust, And factious rage, and breach of trust, And flattery tipped with nauseous fleer, And guilt and shame, and servile fear, Envy, and cruelty, and pride, Will in your tainted heart preside.

Heroes and heroines of old, By honour only were enrolled Among their brethren in the skies, To which (though late) shall Stella rise. Ten thousand oaths upon record Are not so sacred as her word; The world shall in its atoms end Ere Stella can deceive a friend. By honour seated in her breast, She still determines what is best; What indignation in her mind, Against enslavers of mankind! Base kings and ministers of state, Eternal objects of her hate.

She thinks that Nature ne'er designed, Courage to man alone confined; Can cowardice her sex adorn, Which most exposes ours to scorn; She wonders where the charm appears In Florimel's affected fears; For Stella never learned the art At proper times to scream and start; Nor calls up all the house at night, And swears she saw a thing in white. Doll never flies to cut her lace, Or throw cold water in her face, Because she heard a sudden drum, Or found an earwig in a plum.

Her hearers are amazed from whence Proceeds that fund of wit and sense; Which, though her modesty would shroud, Breaks like the sun behind a cloud, While gracefulness its art conceals, And yet through every motion steals.

Say, Stella, was Prometheus blind, And forming you, mistook your kind? No; 'twas for you alone he stole The fire that forms a manly soul; Then, to complete it every way, He moulded it with female clay, To that you owe the nobler flame, To this, the beauty of your frame.

How would ingratitude delight? And how would censure glut her spite? If I should Stella's kindness hide In silence, or forget with pride, When on my sickly couch I lay, Impatient both of night and day, Lamenting in unmanly strains, Called every power to ease my pains, Then Stella ran to my relief With cheerful face and inward grief; And though by Heaven's severe decree She suffers hourly more than me, No cruel master could require, From slaves employed for daily hire, What Stella by her friendship warmed, With vigour and delight performed. My sinking spirits now supplies With cordials in her hands and eyes, Now with a soft and silent tread, Unheard she moves about my bed. I see her taste each nauseous draught, And so obligingly am caught: I bless the hand from whence they came, Nor dare distort my face for shame.

Best pattern of true friends beware, You pay too dearly for your care; If while your tenderness secures My life, it must endanger yours. For such a fool was never found, Who pulled a palace to the ground, Only to have the ruins made Materials for a house decayed.

*While Dr. Swift was at Sir William Temple's, after he left the University of Dublin, he contracted a friendship with two of Sir William's relations, Mrs. Johnson and Mrs. Dingley, which continued to their deaths. The former of these was the amiable Stella, so much celebrated in his works. In the year 1727, being in England, he received the melancholy news of her last sickness, Mrs. Dingley having been dead before. He hastened into Ireland, where he visited her, not only as a friend, but a clergyman. No set form of prayer could express the sense of his heart on that occasion. He drew up the following, here printed from his own handwriting. She died Jan. 28, 1727.*

# THE FIRST HE WROTE OCT. 17, 1727.

Most merciful Father, accept our humblest prayers in behalf of this Thy languishing servant; forgive the sins, the frailties, and infirmities of her life past. Accept the good deeds she hath done in such a manner that, at whatever time Thou shalt please to call her, she may be received into everlasting habitations. Give her grace to continue sincerely thankful to Thee for the many favours Thou hast bestowed upon her, the ability and inclination and practice to do good, and those virtues which have procured the esteem and love of her friends, and a most unspotted name in the world. O God, Thou dispensest Thy blessings and Thy punishments, as it becometh infinite justice and mercy; and since it was Thy pleasure to afflict her with a long, constant, weakly state of health, make her truly sensible that it was for very wise ends, and was largely made up to her in other blessings, more valuable and less common. Continue to her, O Lord, that firmness and constancy of mind wherewith Thou hast most graciously endowed her, together with that contempt of worldly things and vanities that she hath shown in the whole conduct of her life. O All-powerful Being, the least motion of whose Will can create or destroy a world, pity us, the mournful friends of Thy distressed servant, who sink under the weight of her present condition, and the fear of losing the most valuable of our friends; restore her to us, O Lord, if it be Thy gracious Will, or inspire us with constancy and resignation to support ourselves under so heavy an affliction. Restore her, O Lord, for the sake of those poor, who by losing her will be desolate, and those sick, who will not only want her bounty, but her care and tending; or else, in Thy mercy, raise up some other in her place with equal disposition and better abilities. Lessen, O Lord, we beseech thee, her bodily pains, or give her a double strength of mind to support them. And if Thou wilt soon take her to Thyself, turn our thoughts rather upon that felicity which we hope she shall enjoy, than upon that unspeakable loss we shall endure. Let her memory be ever dear unto us, and the example of her many virtues, as far as human infirmity will admit, our constant imitation. Accept, O Lord, these prayers poured from the very bottom of our hearts, in Thy mercy, and for the merits of our blessed Saviour. *Amen*.

# THE SECOND PRAYER WAS WRITTEN NOV. 6, 1727.

O Merciful Father, who never afflictest Thy children but for their own good, and with justice, over which Thy mercy always prevaileth, either to turn them to repentance, or to punish them in the present life, in order to reward them in a better; take pity, we beseech Thee, upon this Thy poor afflicted servant, languishing so long and so grievously under the weight of Thy Hand. Give her strength,

O Lord, to support her weakness, and patience to endure her pains, without repining at Thy correction. Forgive every rash and inconsiderate expression which her anguish may at any time force from her tongue, while her heart continueth in an entire submission to Thy Will. Suppress in her, O Lord, all eager desires of life, and lesson her fears of death, by inspiring into her an humble yet assured hope of Thy mercy. Give her a sincere repentance for all her transgressions and omissions, and a firm resolution to pass the remainder of her life in endeavouring to her utmost to observe all thy precepts. We beseech Thee likewise to compose her thoughts, and preserve to her the use of her memory and reason during the course of her sickness. Give her a true conception of the vanity, folly, and insignificancy of all human things; and strengthen her so as to beget in her a sincere love of Thee in the midst of her sufferings. Accept and impute all her good deeds, and forgive her all those offences against Thee, which she hath sincerely repented of, or through the frailty of memory hath forgot. And now, O Lord, we turn to Thee in behalf of ourselves, and the rest of her sorrowful friends. Let not our grief afflict her mind, and thereby have an ill effect on her present distemper. Forgive the sorrow and weakness of those among us who sink under the grief and terror of losing so dear and useful a friend. Accept and pardon our most earnest prayers and wishes for her longer continuance in this evil world, to do what Thou art pleased to call Thy service, and is only her bounden duty; that she may be still a comfort to us, and to all others, who will want the benefit of her conversation, her advice, her good offices, or her charity. And since Thou hast promised that where two or three are gathered together in Thy Name, Thou wilt be in the midst of them to grant their request, O Gracious Lord, grant to us who are here met in Thy Name, that those requests, which in the utmost sincerity and earnestness of our hearts we have now made in behalf of this Thy distressed servant, and of ourselves, may effectually be answered; through the merits of Jesus Christ our Lord. *Amen*.

# THE BEASTS' CONFESSION (1732).

When beasts could speak (the learned say They still can do so every day), It seems, they had religion then, As much as now we find in men. It happened when a plague broke out (Which therefore made them more devout) The king of brutes (to make it plain, Of quadrupeds I only mean), By proclamation gave command, That every subject in the land Should to the priest confess their sins; And thus the pious wolf begins:

Good father, I must own with shame, That, often I have been to blame: I must confess, on Friday last, Wretch that I was, I broke my fast: But I defy the basest tongue To prove I did my neighbour wrong; Or ever went to seek my food By rapine, theft, or thirst of blood.

The ass approaching next, confessed, That in his heart he loved a jest: A wag he was, he needs must own, And could not let a dunce alone: Sometimes his friend he would not spare, And might perhaps be too severe: But yet, the worst that could be said, He was a wit both born and bred; And, if it be a sin or shame, Nature alone must bear the blame: One fault he hath, is sorry for't, His ears are half a foot too short; Which could he to the standard bring, He'd show his face before the king: Then, for his voice, there's none disputes That he's the nightingale of brutes.

The swine with contrite heart allowed, His shape and beauty made him proud: In diet was perhaps too nice, But gluttony was ne'er his vice: In every turn of life content, And meekly took what fortune sent: Enquire through all the parish round, A better neighbour ne'er was found: His vigilance might seine displease; 'Tis true, he hated sloth like pease.

The mimic ape began his chatter, How evil tongues his life bespatter: Much of the cens'ring world complained, Who said his gravity was feigned: Indeed, the strictness of his morals Engaged him in a hundred quarrels: He saw, and he was grieved to see't, His zeal was sometimes indiscreet: He found his virtues too severe For our corrupted times to bear: Yet, such a lewd licentious age Might well excuse a stoic's rage.

The goat advanced with decent pace: And first excused his youthful face; Forgiveness begged, that he appeared ('Twas nature's fault) without a beard. 'Tis true, he was not much inclined To fondness for the female kind; Not, as his enemies object, From chance or natural defect; Not by his frigid constitution, But through a pious resolution; For he had made a holy vow Of chastity, as monks do now; Which he resolved to keep for ever hence, As strictly, too, as doth his reverence. {5}

Apply the tale, and you shall find How just it suits with human kind. Some faults we own: but, can you guess? Why?--virtue's carried to excess; Wherewith our vanity endows us, Though neither foe nor friend allows us.

The lawyer swears, you may rely on't, He never squeezed a needy client: And this he makes his constant rule, For which his brethren call him fool; His conscience always was so nice, He freely gave the poor advice; By which he lost, he may affirm, A hundred fees last Easter term. While others of the learned robe Would break the patience of a Job; No pleader at the bar could match His diligence and quick despatch; Ne'er kept a cause, he well may boast, Above a term or two at most.

The cringing knave, who seeks a place Without success, thus tells his case: Why should he longer mince the matter? He failed because he could not flatter: He had not learned to turn his coat, Nor for a party give his vote. His crime he quickly understood; Too zealous for the nation's good: He found the ministers resent it, Yet could not for his heart repent it.

The chaplain vows he cannot fawn, Though it would raise him to the lawn: He passed his hours among his books; You find it in his meagre looks: He might, if he were worldly-wise, Preferment get, and spare his eyes: But owned he had a stubborn spirit, That made him trust alone in merit: Would rise by merit to promotion; Alas! a mere chimeric notion.

The doctor, if you will believe him, Confessed a sin, and God forgive him: Called up at midnight, ran to save A blind old beggar from the grave: But, see how Satan spreads his snares; He quite forgot to say his prayers. He cannot help it, for his heart, Sometimes to act the parson's part, Quotes from the Bible many a sentence That moves his patients to repentance: And, when his medicines do no good, Supports their minds with heavenly food. At which, however well intended, He hears the clergy are offended; And grown so bold behind his back, To call him hypocrite and quack. In his own church he keeps a seat; Says grace before and after meat; And calls, without affecting airs, His household twice a day to prayers. He shuns apothecaries' shops; And hates to cram the sick with slops: He scorns to make his art a trade, Nor bribes my lady's favourite maid. Old nurse-keepers would never hire To recommend him to the Squire; Which others, whom he will not name, Have often practised to their shame.

The statesman tells you with a sneer, His fault is to be too sincere; And, having no sinister ends, Is apt to disoblige his friends. The nation's good, his Master's glory,

Without regard to Whig or Tory, Were all the schemes he had in view; Yet he was seconded by few: Though some had spread a thousand lies, 'Twas he defeated the Excise. 'Twas known, though he had borne aspersion, That standing troops were his aversion: His practice was, in every station, To serve the king, and please the nation. Though hard to find in every case The fittest man to fill a place: His promises he ne'er forgot, But took memorials on the spot: His enemies, for want of charity, Said he affected popularity: 'Tis true, the people understood, That all he did was for their good; Their kind affections he has tried; No love is lost on either side. He came to court with fortune clear, Which now he runs out every year; Must, at the rate that he goes on, Inevitably be undone. Oh! if his Majesty would please To give him but a writ of ease, Would grant him license to retire, As it hath long been his desire, By fair accounts it would be found, He's poorer by ten thousand pound. He owns, and hopes it is no sin, He ne'er was partial to his kin; He thought it base for men in stations To crowd the court with their relations: His country was his dearest mother, And every virtuous man his brother: Through modesty or awkward shame (For which he owns himself to blame), He found the wisest men he could, Without respect to friends or blood; Nor never acts on private views, When he hath liberty to choose.

The sharper swore he hated play, Except to pass an hour away: And well he might; for to his cost, By want of skill, he always lost. He heard there was a club of cheats, Who had contrived a thousand feats; Could change the stock, or cog a dye, And thus deceive the sharpest eye: No wonder how his fortune sunk, His brothers fleece him when he's drunk.

I own the moral not exact; Besides, the tale is false in fact; And so absurd, that, could I raise up From fields Elysian, fabling AEsop; I would accuse him to his face, For libelling the four-foot race. Creatures of every kind but ours Well comprehend their natural powers; While we, whom reason ought to sway, Mistake our talents every day: The ass was never known so stupid To act the part of Tray or Cupid; Nor leaps upon his master's lap, There to be stroked, and fed with pap: As AEsop would the world persuade; He better understands his trade: Nor comes whene'er his lady whistles, But carries loads, and feeds on thistles; Our author's meaning, I presume, is A creature *bipes et implumis*; Wherein the moralist designed A compliment on human-kind: For, here he owns, that now and then Beasts may degenerate into men.

AN ARGUMENT TO PROVE THAT THE ABOLISHING OF CHRISTIANITY
IN ENGLAND MAY, AS THINGS NOW STAND, BE ATTENDED WITH SOME
INCONVENIENCES, AND PERHAPS NOT PRODUCE THOSE MANY GOOD
EFFECTS PROPOSED THEREBY.

### *Written in the year 1708*.

I am very sensible what a weakness and presumption it is to reason against the
general humour and disposition of the world. I remember it was with great justice,
and a due regard to the freedom, both of the public and the press, forbidden upon
several penalties to write, or discourse, or lay wagers against the --- even before it
was confirmed by Parliament; because that was looked upon as a design to oppose
the current of the people, which, besides the folly of it, is a manifest breach of the
fundamental law, that makes this majority of opinions the voice of God. In like
manner, and for the very same reasons, it may perhaps be neither safe nor prudent
to argue against the abolishing of Christianity, at a juncture when all parties seem so
unanimously determined upon the point, as we cannot but allow from their actions,
their discourses, and their writings. However, I know not how, whether from the
affectation of singularity, or the perverseness of human nature, but so it unhappily
falls out, that I cannot be entirely of this opinion. Nay, though I were sure an order
were issued for my immediate prosecution by the Attorney-General, I should still
confess, that in the present posture of our affairs at home or abroad, I do not yet see
the absolute necessity of extirpating the Christian religion from among us.

This perhaps may appear too great a paradox even for our wise and paxodoxical
age to endure; therefore I shall handle it with all tenderness, and with the utmost
deference to that great and profound majority which is of another sentiment.

And yet the curious may please to observe, how much the genius of a nation is
liable to alter in half an age. I have heard it affirmed for certain by some very odd
people, that the contrary opinion was even in their memories as much in vogue as
the other is now; and that a project for the abolishing of Christianity would then
have appeared as singular, and been thought as absurd, as it would be at this time to
write or discourse in its defence.

Therefore I freely own, that all appearances are against me. The system of the Gospel, after the fate of other systems, is generally antiquated and exploded, and the mass or body of the common people, among whom it seems to have had its latest credit, are now grown as much ashamed of it as their betters; opinions, like fashions, always descending from those of quality to the middle sort, and thence to the vulgar, where at length they are dropped and vanish.

But here I would not be mistaken, and must therefore be so bold as to borrow a distinction from the writers on the other side, when they make a difference betwixt nominal and real Trinitarians. I hope no reader imagines me so weak to stand up in the defence of real Christianity, such as used in primitive times (if we may believe the authors of those ages) to have an influence upon men's belief and actions. To offer at the restoring of that, would indeed be a wild project: it would be to dig up foundations; to destroy at one blow all the wit, and half the learning of the kingdom; to break the entire frame and constitution of things; to ruin trade, extinguish arts and sciences, with the professors of them; in short, to turn our courts, exchanges, and shops into deserts; and would be full as absurd as the proposal of Horace, where he advises the Romans, all in a body, to leave their city, and seek a new seat in some remote part of the world, by way of a cure for the corruption of their manners.

Therefore I think this caution was in itself altogether unnecessary (which I have inserted only to prevent all possibility of cavilling), since every candid reader will easily understand my discourse to be intended only in defence of nominal Christianity, the other having been for some time wholly laid aside by general consent, as utterly inconsistent with all our present schemes of wealth and power.

But why we should therefore cut off the name and title of Christians, although the general opinion and resolution be so violent for it, I confess I cannot (with submission) apprehend the consequence necessary. However, since the undertakers propose such wonderful advantages to the nation by this project, and advance many plausible objections against the system of Christianity, I shall briefly consider the strength of both, fairly allow them their greatest weight, and offer such answers as I think most reasonable. After which I will beg leave to show what inconveniences may possibly happen by such an innovation, in the present posture of our affairs.

First, one great advantage proposed by the abolishing of Christianity is, that it would very much enlarge and establish liberty of conscience, that great bulwark of our nation, and of the Protestant religion, which is still too much limited by priestcraft, notwithstanding all the good intentions of the legislature, as we have lately found by a severe instance. For it is confidently reported, that two young gentlemen of real hopes, bright wit, and profound judgment, who, upon a thorough examination of causes and effects, and by the mere force of natural abilities, without the least tincture of learning, having made a discovery that there was no God, and generously communicating their thoughts for the good of the public, were some time ago, by an unparalleled severity, and upon I know not what obsolete law, broke for blasphemy. And as it has been wisely observed, if persecution once begins, no man alive knows how far it may reach, or where it will end.

In answer to all which, with deference to wiser judgments, I think this rather shows the necessity of a nominal religion among us. Great wits love to be free with the highest objects; and if they cannot be allowed a god to revile or renounce, they will speak evil of dignities, abuse the government, and reflect upon the ministry, which I am sure few will deny to be of much more pernicious consequence, according to the saying of Tiberius, ***deorum offensa diis curoe***. As to the particular fact related, I think it is not fair to argue from one instance, perhaps another cannot be produced: yet (to the comfort of all those who may be apprehensive of persecution) blasphemy we know is freely spoke a million of times in every coffee-house and tavern, or wherever else good company meet. It must be allowed, indeed, that to break an English free-born officer only for blasphemy was, to speak the gentlest of such an action, a very high strain of absolute power. Little can be said in excuse for the general; perhaps he was afraid it might give offence to the allies, among whom, for aught we know, it may be the custom of the country to believe a God. But if he argued, as some have done, upon a mistaken principle, that an officer who is guilty of speaking blasphemy may, some time or other, proceed so far as to raise a mutiny, the consequence is by no means to be admitted: for surely the commander of an English army is like to be but ill obeyed whose soldiers fear and reverence him as little as they do a Deity.

It is further objected against the Gospel system that it obliges men to the belief of things too difficult for Freethinkers, and such who have shook off the prejudices that usually cling to a confined education. To which I answer, that men should be cautious how they raise objections which reflect upon the wisdom of the nation. Is not everybody freely allowed to believe whatever he pleases, and to publish his belief to the world whenever he thinks fit, especially if it serves to strengthen the party which is in the right? Would any indifferent foreigner, who should read the trumpery lately written by Asgil, Tindal, Toland, Coward, and forty more, imagine the Gospel to be our rule of faith, and to be confirmed by Parliaments? Does any man either believe, or say he believes, or desire to have it thought that he says he believes, one syllable of the matter? And is any man worse received upon that score, or does he find his want of nominal faith a disadvantage to him in the pursuit of any civil or military employment? What if there be an old dormant statute or two against him, are they not now obsolete, to a degree, that Empson and Dudley themselves, if they were now alive, would find it impossible to put them in execution?

It is likewise urged, that there are, by computation, in this kingdom, above ten thousand parsons, whose revenues, added to those of my lords the bishops, would suffice to maintain at least two hundred young gentlemen of wit and pleasure, and free-thinking, enemies to priestcraft, narrow principles, pedantry, and prejudices, who might be an ornament to the court and town: and then again, so a great number of able [bodied] divines might be a recruit to our fleet and armies. This indeed appears to be a consideration of some weight; but then, on the other side, several things deserve to be considered likewise: as, first, whether it may not be thought necessary that in certain tracts of country, like what we call parishes, there should be one man at least of abilities to read and write. Then it seems a wrong computation that the revenues of the Church throughout this island would be large enough to maintain two hundred young gentlemen, or even half that number, after the present refined way of living, that is, to allow each of them such a rent as, in the modern form of speech, would make them easy. But still there is in this project a greater mischief behind; and we ought to beware of the woman's folly, who killed the hen that every morning laid her a golden egg. For, pray what would become of the race of men in the next age, if we had nothing to trust to beside the scrofulous consumptive production furnished by our men of wit and pleasure, when, having squandered away their vigour, health, and estates, they are forced, by some disagreeable marriage, to piece up their broken fortunes, and entail rottenness and politeness on their posterity? Now, here are ten thousand persons reduced, by the wise regulations of Henry VIII., to the necessity of a low diet, and moderate exercise, who are the only great restorers of our breed, without which the nation would in an age or two become one great hospital.

Another advantage proposed by the abolishing of Christianity is the clear gain of one day in seven, which is now entirely lost, and consequently the kingdom one seventh less considerable in trade, business, and pleasure; besides the loss to the public of so many stately structures now in the hands of the clergy, which might be converted into play-houses, exchanges, market-houses, common dormitories, and other public edifices.

I hope I shall be forgiven a hard word if I call this a perfect cavil. I readily own there hath been an old custom, time out of mind, for people to assemble in the churches every Sunday, and that shops are still frequently shut, in order, as it is conceived, to preserve the memory of that ancient practice; but how this can prove a hindrance to business or pleasure is hard to imagine. What if the men of pleasure are forced, one day in the week, to game at home instead of the chocolate-house? Are not the taverns and coffee-houses open? Can there be a more convenient season for taking a dose of physic? Is not that the chief day for traders to sum up the accounts of the week, and for lawyers to prepare their briefs? But I would fain know how it can be pretended that the churches are misapplied? Where are more appointments and rendezvouses of gallantry? Where more care to appear in the foremost box, with greater advantage of dress? Where more meetings for business? Where more bargains driven of all sorts? And where so many conveniences or incitements to sleep?

There is one advantage greater than any of the foregoing, proposed by the abolishing of Christianity, that it will utterly extinguish parties among us, by removing those factious distinctions of high and low church, of Whig and Tory, Presbyterian and Church of England, which are now so many mutual clogs upon public proceedings, and are apt to prefer the gratifying themselves or depressing their adversaries before the most important interest of the State.

I confess, if it were certain that so great an advantage would redound to the nation by this expedient, I would submit, and be silent; but will any man say, that if the words, whoring, drinking, cheating, lying, stealing, were, by Act of Parliament, ejected out of the English tongue and dictionaries, we should all awake next morning chaste and temperate, honest and just, and lovers of truth?  Is this a fair consequence?  Or if the physicians would forbid us to pronounce the words pox, gout, rheumatism, and stone, would that expedient serve like so many talismens to destroy the diseases themselves?  Are party and faction rooted in men's hearts no deeper than phrases borrowed from religion, or founded upon no firmer principles?  And is our language so poor that we cannot find other terms to express them?  Are envy, pride, avarice, and ambition such ill nomenclators, that they cannot furnish appellations for their owners?  Will not heydukes and mamalukes, mandarins and patshaws, or any other words formed at pleasure, serve to distinguish those who are in the ministry from others who would be in it if they could?  What, for instance, is easier than to vary the form of speech, and instead of the word church, make it a question in politics, whether the monument be in danger?  Because religion was nearest at hand to furnish a few convenient phrases, is our invention so barren we can find no other?  Suppose, for argument sake, that the Tories favoured Margarita, the Whigs, Mrs. Tofts, and the Trimmers, Valentini, would not Margaritians, Toftians, and Valentinians be very tolerable marks of distinction?  The Prasini and Veniti, two most virulent factions in Italy, began, if I remember right, by a distinction of colours in ribbons, which we might do with as good a grace about the dignity of the blue and the green, and serve as properly to divide the Court, the Parliament, and the kingdom between them, as any terms of art whatsoever, borrowed from religion.  And therefore I think there is little force in this objection against Christianity, or prospect of so great an advantage as is proposed in the abolishing of it.

It is again objected, as a very absurd, ridiculous custom, that a set of men should be suffered, much less employed and hired, to bawl one day in seven against the lawfulness of those methods most in use towards the pursuit of greatness, riches, and pleasure, which are the constant practice of all men alive on the other six.  But this objection is, I think, a little unworthy so refined an age as ours.  Let us argue this matter calmly.  I appeal to the breast of any polite Free-thinker, whether, in the pursuit of gratifying a pre-dominant passion, he hath not always felt a wonderful incitement, by reflecting it was a thing forbidden; and therefore we see, in order to cultivate this test, the wisdom of the nation hath taken special care that the ladies should be furnished with prohibited silks, and the men with prohibited wine.  And indeed it were to be wished that some other prohibitions were promoted, in order to improve the pleasures of the town, which, for want of such expedients, begin already, as I am told, to flag and grow languid, giving way daily to cruel inroads from the spleen.

'Tis likewise proposed, as a great advantage to the public, that if we once discard the system of the Gospel, all religion will of course be banished for ever, and consequently along with it those grievous prejudices of education which, under the names of conscience, honour, justice, and the like, are so apt to disturb the peace of human minds, and the notions whereof are so hard to be eradicated by right reason or free-thinking, sometimes during the whole course of our lives.

Here first I observe how difficult it is to get rid of a phrase which the world has once grown fond of, though the occasion that first produced it be entirely taken away. For some years past, if a man had but an ill- favoured nose, the deep thinkers of the age would, some way or other contrive to impute the cause to the prejudice of his education. From this fountain were said to be derived all our foolish notions of justice, piety, love of our country; all our opinions of God or a future state, heaven, hell, and the like; and there might formerly perhaps have been some pretence for this charge. But so effectual care hath been since taken to remove those prejudices, by an entire change in the methods of education, that (with honour I mention it to our polite innovators) the young gentlemen, who are now on the scene, seem to have not the least tincture left of those infusions, or string of those weeds, and by consequence the reason for abolishing nominal Christianity upon that pretext is wholly ceased.

For the rest, it may perhaps admit a controversy, whether the banishing all notions of religion whatsoever would be inconvenient for the vulgar. Not that I am in the least of opinion with those who hold religion to have been the invention of politicians, to keep the lower part of the world in awe by the fear of invisible powers; unless mankind were then very different from what it is now; for I look upon the mass or body of our people here in England to be as Freethinkers, that is to say, as staunch unbelievers, as any of the highest rank. But I conceive some scattered notions about a superior power to be of singular use for the common people, as furnishing excellent materials to keep children quiet when they grow peevish, and providing topics of amusement in a tedious winter night.

Lastly, it is proposed, as a singular advantage, that the abolishing of Christianity will very much contribute to the uniting of Protestants, by enlarging the terms of communion, so as to take in all sorts of Dissenters, who are now shut out of the pale upon account of a few ceremonies, which all sides confess to be things indifferent. That this alone will effectually answer the great ends of a scheme for comprehension, by opening a large noble gate, at which all bodies may enter; whereas the chaffering with Dissenters, and dodging about this or t'other ceremony, is but like opening a few wickets, and leaving them at jar, by which no more than one can get in at a time, and that not without stooping, and sideling, and squeezing his body.

To all this I answer, that there is one darling inclination of mankind which usually affects to be a retainer to religion, though she be neither its parent, its godmother, nor its friend. I mean the spirit of opposition, that lived long before Christianity, and can easily subsist without it. Let us, for instance, examine wherein the opposition of sectaries among us consists. We shall find Christianity to have no share in it at all. Does the Gospel anywhere prescribe a starched, squeezed countenance, a stiff formal gait, a singularity of manners and habit, or any affected forms and modes of speech different from the reasonable part of mankind? Yet, if Christianity did not lend its name to stand in the gap, and to employ or divert these humours, they must of necessity be spent in contraventions to the laws of the land, and disturbance of the public peace. There is a portion of enthusiasm assigned to every nation, which, if it hath not proper objects to work on, will burst out, and set all into a flame. If the quiet of a State can be bought by only flinging men a few ceremonies to devour, it is a purchase no wise man would refuse. Let the mastiffs amuse themselves about a sheep's skin stuffed with hay, provided it will keep them from worrying the flock. The institution of convents abroad seems in one point a strain of great wisdom, there being few irregularities in human passions which may not have recourse to vent themselves in some of those orders, which are so many retreats for the speculative, the melancholy, the proud, the silent, the politic, and the morose, to spend themselves, and evaporate the noxious particles; for each of whom we in this island are forced to provide a several sect of religion to keep them quiet; and whenever Christianity shall be abolished, the Legislature must find some other expedient to employ and entertain them. For what imports it how large a gate you open, if there will be always left a number who place a pride and a merit in not coming in?

Having thus considered the most important objections against Christianity, and the chief advantages proposed by the abolishing thereof, I shall now, with equal deference and submission to wiser judgments, as before, proceed to mention a few inconveniences that may happen if the Gospel should be repealed, which, perhaps, the projectors may not have sufficiently considered.

And first, I am very sensible how much the gentlemen of wit and pleasure are apt to murmur, and be choked at the sight of so many daggle-tailed parsons that happen to fall in their way, and offend their eyes; but at the same time, these wise reformers do not consider what an advantage and felicity it is for great wits to be always provided with objects of scorn and contempt, in order to exercise and improve their talents, and divert their spleen from falling on each other, or on themselves, especially when all this may be done without the least imaginable danger to their persons.

And to urge another argument of a parallel nature: if Christianity were once abolished, how could the Freethinkers, the strong reasoners, and the men of profound learning be able to find another subject so calculated in all points whereon to display their abilities? What wonderful productions of wit should we be deprived of from those whose genius, by continual practice, hath been wholly turned upon raillery and invectives against religion, and would therefore never be able to shine or distinguish themselves upon any other subject? We are daily complaining of the great decline of wit among as, and would we take away the greatest, perhaps the only topic we have left? Who would ever have suspected Asgil for a wit, or Toland for a philosopher, if the inexhaustible stock of Christianity had not been at hand to provide them with materials? What other subject through all art or nature could have produced Tindal for a profound author, or furnished him with readers? It is the wise choice of the subject that alone adorns and distinguishes the writer. For had a hundred such pens as these been employed on the side of religion, they would have immediately sunk into silence and oblivion.

Nor do I think it wholly groundless, or my fears altogether imaginary, that the abolishing of Christianity may perhaps bring the Church in danger, or at least put the Senate to the trouble of another securing vote. I desire I may not be mistaken; I am far from presuming to affirm or think that the Church is in danger at present, or as things now stand; but we know not how soon it may be so when the Christian religion is repealed.  As plausible as this project seems, there may be a dangerous design lurk under it.  Nothing can be more notorious than that the Atheists, Deists, Socinians, Anti-Trinitarians, and other subdivisions of Freethinkers, are persons of little zeal for the present ecclesiastical establishment: their declared opinion is for repealing the sacramental test; they are very indifferent with regard to ceremonies; nor do they hold the *Jus Divinum* of episcopacy: therefore they may be intended as one politic step towards altering the constitution of the Church established, and setting up Presbytery in the stead, which I leave to be further considered by those at the helm.

In the last place, I think nothing can be more plain, than that by this expedient we shall run into the evil we chiefly pretend to avoid; and that the abolishment of the Christian religion will be the readiest course we can take to introduce Popery. And I am the more inclined to this opinion because we know it has been the constant practice of the Jesuits to send over emissaries, with instructions to personate themselves members of the several prevailing sects amongst us.  So it is recorded that they have at sundry times appeared in the guise of Presbyterians, Anabaptists, Independents, and Quakers, according as any of these were most in credit; so, since the fashion hath been taken up of exploding religion, the Popish missionaries have not been wanting to mix with the Freethinkers; among whom Toland, the great oracle of the Anti- Christians, is an Irish priest, the son of an Irish priest; and the most learned and ingenious author of a book called the "Rights of the Christian Church," was in a proper juncture reconciled to the Romish faith, whose true son, as appears by a hundred passages in his treatise, he still continues.  Perhaps I could add some others to the number; but the fact is beyond dispute, and the reasoning they proceed by is right: for supposing Christianity to be extinguished the people will never he at ease till they find out some other method of worship, which will as infallibly produce superstition as this will end in Popery.

And therefore, if, notwithstanding all I have said, it still be thought necessary to have a Bill brought in for repealing Christianity, I would humbly offer an amendment, that instead of the word Christianity may be put religion in general, which I conceive will much better answer all the good ends proposed by the projectors of it.  For as long as we leave in being a God and His Providence, with all the necessary consequences which curious and inquisitive men will be apt to draw from such promises, we do not strike at the root of the evil, though we should ever so effectually annihilate the present scheme of the Gospel; for of what use is freedom of thought if it will not produce freedom of action, which is the sole end, how remote soever in appearance, of all objections against Christianity? and therefore, the Freethinkers consider it as a sort of edifice, wherein all the parts have such a mutual dependence on each other, that if you happen to pull out one single nail, the whole fabric must fall to the ground. This was happily expressed by him who had heard of a text brought for proof of the Trinity, which in an ancient manuscript was differently read; he thereupon immediately took the hint, and by a sudden deduction of a long Sorites, most logically concluded: why, if it be as you say, I may safely drink on, and defy the parson. From which, and many the like instances easy to be produced, I think nothing can be more manifest than that the quarrel is not against any particular points of hard digestion in the Christian system, but against religion in general, which, by laying restraints on human nature, is supposed the great enemy to the freedom of thought and action.

Upon the whole, if it shall still be thought for the benefit of Church and State that Christianity be abolished, I conceive, however, it may be more convenient to defer the execution to a time of peace, and not venture in this conjuncture to disoblige our allies, who, as it falls out, are all Christians, and many of them, by the prejudices of their education, so bigoted as to place a sort of pride in the appellation. If, upon being rejected by them, we are to trust to an alliance with the Turk, we shall find ourselves much deceived; for, as he is too remote, and generally engaged in war with the Persian emperor, so his people would be more scandalised at our infidelity than our Christian neighbours. For they are not only strict observers of religions worship, but what is worse, believe a God; which is more than is required of us, even while we preserve the name of Christians.

To conclude, whatever some may think of the great advantages to trade by this favourite scheme, I do very much apprehend that in six months' time after the Act is passed for the extirpation of the Gospel, the Bank and East India stock may fall at least one per cent. And since that is fifty times more than ever the wisdom of our age thought fit to venture for the preservation of Christianity, there is no reason we should be at so great a loss merely for the sake of destroying it.

# HINTS TOWARDS AN ESSAY ON CONVERSATION.

I have observed few obvious subjects to have been so seldom, or at least so slightly, handled as this; and, indeed, I know few so difficult to be treated as it ought, nor yet upon which there seemeth so much to be said.

Most things pursued by men for the happiness of public or private life our wit or folly have so refined, that they seldom subsist but in idea; a true friend, a good marriage, a perfect form of government, with some others, require so many ingredients, so good in their several kinds, and so much niceness in mixing them, that for some thousands of years men have despaired of reducing their schemes to perfection. But in conversation it is or might be otherwise; for here we are only to avoid a multitude of errors, which, although a matter of some difficulty, may be in every man's power, for want of which it remaineth as mere an idea as the other. Therefore it seemeth to me that the truest way to understand conversation is to know the faults and errors to which it is subject, and from thence every man to form maxims to himself whereby it may be regulated, because it requireth few talents to which most men are not born, or at least may not acquire without any great genius or study. For nature bath left every man a capacity of being agreeable, though not of shining in company; and there are a hundred men sufficiently qualified for both, who, by a very few faults that they might correct in half an hour, are not so much as tolerable.

I was prompted to write my thoughts upon this subject by mere indignation, to reflect that so useful and innocent a pleasure, so fitted for every period and condition of life, and so much in all men's power, should be so much neglected and abused.

And in this discourse it will be necessary to note those errors that are obvious, as well as others which are seldomer observed, since there are few so obvious or acknowledged into which most men, some time or other, are not apt to run.

For instance, nothing is more generally exploded than the folly of talking too much; yet I rarely remember to have seen five people together where some one among them hath not been predominant in that kind, to the great constraint and disgust of all the rest. But among such as deal in multitudes of words, none are comparable to the sober deliberate talker, who proceedeth with much thought and caution, maketh his preface, brancheth out into several digressions, findeth a hint that putteth him in mind of another story, which he promiseth to tell you when this is done; cometh back regularly to his subject, cannot readily call to mind some person's name, holdeth his head, complaineth of his memory; the whole company all this while in suspense; at length, says he, it is no matter, and so goes on. And, to crown the business, it perhaps proveth at last a story the company hath heard fifty times before; or, at best, some insipid adventure of the relater.

Another general fault in conversation is that of those who affect to talk of themselves. Some, without any ceremony, will run over the history of their lives; will relate the annals of their diseases, with the several symptoms and circumstances of them; will enumerate the hardships and injustice they have suffered in court, in parliament, in love, or in law. Others are more dexterous, and with great art will lie on the watch to hook in their own praise. They will call a witness to remember they always foretold what would happen in such a case, but none would believe them; they advised such a man from the beginning, and told him the consequences just as they happened, but he would have his own way. Others make a vanity of telling their faults. They are the strangest men in the world; they cannot dissemble; they own it is a folly; they have lost abundance of advantages by it; but, if you would give them the world, they cannot help it; there is something in their nature that abhors insincerity and constraint; with many other unsufferable topics of the same altitude.

Of such mighty importance every man is to himself, and ready to think he is so to others, without once making this easy and obvious reflection, that his affairs can have no more weight with other men than theirs have with him; and how little that is he is sensible enough.

Where company hath met, I often have observed two persons discover by some accident that they were bred together at the same school or university, after which the rest are condemned to silence, and to listen while these two are refreshing each other's memory with the arch tricks and passages of themselves and their comrades.

I know a great officer of the army, who will sit for some time with a supercilious and impatient silence, full of anger and contempt for those who are talking; at length of a sudden demand audience; decide the matter in a short dogmatical way; then withdraw within himself again, and vouchsafe to talk no more, until his spirits circulate again to the same point.

There are some faults in conversation which none are so subject to as the men of wit, nor ever so much as when they are with each other. If they have opened their mouths without endeavouring to say a witty thing, they think it is so many words lost. It is a torment to the hearers, as much as to themselves, to see them upon the rack for invention, and in perpetual constraint, with so little success. They must do something extraordinary, in order to acquit themselves, and answer their character, else the standers by may be disappointed and be apt to think them only like the rest of mortals. I have known two men of wit industriously brought together, in order to entertain the company, where they have made a very ridiculous figure, and provided all the mirth at their own expense.

I know a man of wit, who is never easy but where he can be allowed to dictate and preside; he neither expecteth to be informed or entertained, but to display his own talents. His business is to be good company, and not good conversation, and therefore he chooseth to frequent those who are content to listen, and profess themselves his admirers. And, indeed, the worst conversation I ever remember to have heard in my life was that at Will's coffee-house, where the wits, as they were called, used formerly to assemble; that is to say, five or six men who had written plays, or at least prologues, or had share in a miscellany, came thither, and entertained one another with their trifling composures in so important an air, as if they had been the noblest efforts of human nature, or that the fate of kingdoms depended on them; and they were usually attended with a humble audience of young students from the inns of courts, or the universities, who, at due distance, listened to these oracles, and returned home with great contempt for their law and philosophy, their heads filled with trash under the name of politeness, criticism, and belles lettres.

By these means the poets, for many years past, were all overrun with pedantry. For, as I take it, the word is not properly used; because pedantry is the too front or unseasonable obtruding our own knowledge in common discourse, and placing too great a value upon it; by which definition men of the court or the army may be as guilty of pedantry as a philosopher or a divine; and it is the same vice in women when they are over copious upon the subject of their petticoats, or their fans, or their china. For which reason, although it be a piece of prudence, as well as good manners, to put men upon talking on subjects they are best versed in, yet that is a liberty a wise man could hardly take; because, beside the imputation of pedantry, it is what he would never improve by.

This great town is usually provided with some player, mimic, or buffoon, who hath a general reception at the good tables; familiar and domestic with persons of the first quality, and usually sent for at every meeting to divert the company, against which I have no objection. You go there as to a farce or a puppet-show; your business is only to laugh in season, either out of inclination or civility, while this merry companion is acting his part. It is a business he hath undertaken, and we are to suppose he is paid for his day's work. I only quarrel when in select and private meetings, where men of wit and learning are invited to pass an evening, this jester should be admitted to run over his circle of tricks, and make the whole company unfit for any other conversation, besides the indignity of confounding men's talents at so shameful a rate.

Raillery is the finest part of conversation; but, as it is our usual custom to counterfeit and adulterate whatever is too dear for us, so we have done with this, and turned it all into what is generally called repartee, or being smart; just as when an expensive fashion cometh up, those who are not able to reach it content themselves with some paltry imitation. It now passeth for raillery to run a man down in discourse, to put him out of countenance, and make him ridiculous, sometimes to expose the defects of his person or understanding; on all which occasions he is obliged not to be angry, to avoid the imputation of not being able to take a jest. It is admirable to observe one who is dexterous at this art, singling out a weak adversary, getting the laugh on his side, and then carrying all before him. The French, from whom we borrow the word, have a quite different idea of the thing, and so had we in the politer age of our fathers. Raillery was, to say something that at first appeared a reproach or reflection, but, by some turn of wit unexpected and surprising, ended always in a compliment, and to the advantage of the person it was addressed to. And surely one of the best rules in conversation is, never to say a thing which any of the company can reasonably wish we had rather left unsaid; nor can there anything be well more contrary to the ends for which people meet together, than to part unsatisfied with each other or themselves.

There are two faults in conversation which appear very different, yet arise from the same root, and are equally blamable; I mean, an impatience to interrupt others, and the uneasiness of being interrupted ourselves. The two chief ends of conversation are, to entertain and improve those we are among, or to receive those benefits ourselves; which whoever will consider, cannot easily run into either of those two errors; because, when any man speaketh in company, it is to be supposed he doth it for his hearers' sake, and not his own; so that common discretion will teach us not to force their attention, if they are not willing to lend it; nor, on the other side, to interrupt him who is in possession, because that is in the grossest manner to give the preference to our own good sense.

There are some people whose good manners will not suffer them to interrupt you; but, what is almost as bad, will discover abundance of impatience, and lie upon the watch until you have done, because they have started something in their own thoughts which they long to be delivered of. Meantime, they are so far from regarding what passes, that their imaginations are wholly turned upon what they have in reserve, for fear it should slip out of their memory; and thus they confine their invention, which might otherwise range over a hundred things full as good, and that might be much more naturally introduced.

There is a sort of rude familiarity, which some people, by practising among their intimates, have introduced into their general conversation, and would have it pass for innocent freedom or humour, which is a dangerous experiment in our northern climate, where all the little decorum and politeness we have are purely forced by art, and are so ready to lapse into barbarity. This, among the Romans, was the raillery of slaves, of which we have many instances in Plautus. It seemeth to have been introduced among us by Cromwell, who, by preferring the scum of the people, made it a court-entertainment, of which I have heard many particulars; and, considering all things were turned upside down, it was reasonable and judicious; although it was a piece of policy found out to ridicule a point of honour in the other extreme, when the smallest word misplaced among gentlemen ended in a duel.

There are some men excellent at telling a story, and provided with a plentiful stock of them, which they can draw out upon occasion in all companies; and considering how low conversation runs now among us, it is not altogether a contempt-ible talent; however, it is subject to two unavoidable defects: frequent repetition, and being soon exhausted; so that whoever valueth this gift in himself hath need of a good memory, and ought frequently to shift his company, that he may not dis-cover the weakness of his fund; for those who are thus endowed have seldom any other revenue, but live upon the main stock.

Great speakers in public are seldom agreeable in private conversation, whether their faculty be natural, or acquired by practice and often venturing. Natural elocu-tion, although it may seem a paradox, usually springeth from a barrenness of inven-tion and of words, by which men who have only one stock of notions upon every subject, and one set of phrases to express them in, they swim upon the superficies, and offer themselves on every occasion; therefore, men of much learning, and who know the compass of a language, are generally the worst talkers on a sudden, until much practice hath inured and emboldened them; because they are confounded with plenty of matter, variety of notions, and of words, which they cannot readily choose, but are perplexed and entangled by too great a choice, which is no disad-vantage in private conversation; where, on the other side, the talent of haranguing is, of all others, most insupportable.

Nothing hath spoiled men more for conversation than the character of being wits; to support which, they never fail of encouraging a number of followers and admirers, who list themselves in their service, wherein they find their accounts on both sides by pleasing their mutual vanity. This hath given the former such an air of superiority, and made the latter so pragmatical, that neither of them are well to be endured. I say nothing here of the itch of dispute and contradiction, telling of lies, or of those who are troubled with the disease called the wandering of the thoughts, that they are never present in mind at what passeth in discourse; for who-ever labours under any of these possessions is as unfit for conversation as madmen in Bedlam.

I think I have gone over most of the errors in conversation that have fallen under my notice or memory, except some that are merely personal, and others too gross to need exploding; such as lewd or profane talk; but I pretend only to treat the errors of conversation in general, and not the several subjects of discourse, which would be infinite. Thus we see how human nature is most debased, by the abuse of that faculty, which is held the great distinction between men and brutes; and how little advantage we make of that which might be the greatest, the most lasting, and the most innocent, as well as useful pleasure of life: in default of which, we are forced to take up with those poor amusements of dress and visiting, or the more pernicious ones of play, drink, and vicious amours, whereby the nobility and gentry of both sexes are entirely corrupted both in body and mind, and have lost all notions of love, honour, friendship, and generosity; which, under the name of fopperies, have been for some time laughed out of doors.

This degeneracy of conversation, with the pernicious consequences thereof upon our humours and dispositions, hath been owing, among other causes, to the custom arisen, for some time past, of excluding women from any share in our society, further than in parties at play, or dancing, or in the pursuit of an amour. I take the highest period of politeness in England (and it is of the same date in France) to have been the peaceable part of King Charles I.'s reign; and from what we read of those times, as well as from the accounts I have formerly met with from some who lived in that court, the methods then used for raising and cultivating conversation were altogether different from ours; several ladies, whom we find celebrated by the poets of that age, had assemblies at their houses, where persons of the best understanding, and of both sexes, met to pass the evenings in discoursing upon whatever agreeable subjects were occasionally started; and although we are apt to ridicule the sublime Platonic notions they had, or personated in love and friendship, I conceive their refinements were grounded upon reason, and that a little grain of the romance is no ill ingredient to preserve and exalt the dignity of human nature, without which it is apt to degenerate into everything that is sordid, vicious, and low. If there were no other use in the conversation of ladies, it is sufficient that it would lay a restraint upon those odious topics of immodesty and indecencies, into which the rudeness of our northern genius is so apt to fall. And, therefore, it is observable in those sprightly gentlemen about the town, who are so very dexterous at entertaining a vizard mask in the park or the playhouse, that, in the company of ladies of virtue and honour, they are silent and disconcerted, and out of their element.

There are some people who think they sufficiently acquit themselves and entertain their company with relating of facts of no consequence, nor at all out of the road of such common incidents as happen every day; and this I have observed more frequently among the Scots than any other nation, who are very careful not to omit the minutest circumstances of time or place; which kind of discourse, if it were not a little relieved by the uncouth terms and phrases, as well as accent and gesture peculiar to that country, would be hardly tolerable. It is not a fault in company to talk much; but to continue it long is certainly one; for, if the majority of those who are got together be naturally silent or cautious, the conversation will flag, unless it be often renewed by one among them who can start new subjects, provided he doth not dwell upon them, but leaveth room for answers and replies.

# THOUGHTS ON VARIOUS SUBJECTS.

We have just enough religion to make us hate, but not enough to make us love one another.

Reflect on things past as wars, negotiations, factions, etc. We enter so little into those interests, that we wonder how men could possibly be so busy and concerned for things so transitory; look on the present times, we find the same humour, yet wonder not at all.

A wise man endeavours, by considering all circumstances, to make conjectures and form conclusions; but the smallest accident intervening (and in the course of affairs it is impossible to foresee all) does often produce such turns and changes, that at last he is just as much in doubt of events as the most ignorant and inexperienced person.

Positiveness is a good quality for preachers and orators, because he that would obtrude his thoughts and reasons upon a multitude, will convince others the more, as he appears convinced himself.

How is it possible to expect that mankind will take advice, when they will not so much as take warning?

I forget whether Advice be among the lost things which Aristo says are to be found in the moon; that and Time ought to have been there.

No preacher is listened to but Time, which gives us the same train and turn of thought that older people have tried in vain to put into our heads before.

When we desire or solicit anything, our minds run wholly on the good side or circumstances of it; when it is obtained, our minds run wholly on the bad ones.

In a glass-house the workmen often fling in a small quantity of fresh coals, which seems to disturb the fire, but very much enlivens it. This seems to allude to a gentle stirring of the passions, that the mind may not languish.

Religion seems to have grown an infant with age, and requires miracles to nurse it, as it had in its infancy.

All fits of pleasure are balanced by an equal degree of pain or languor; it is like spending this year part of the next year's revenue.

The latter part of a wise man's life is taken up in curing the follies, prejudices, and false opinions he had contracted in the former.

Would a writer know how to behave himself with relation to posterity, let him consider in old books what he finds that he is glad to know, and what omissions he most laments.

Whatever the poets pretend, it is plain they give immortality to none but themselves; it is Homer and Virgil we reverence and admire, not Achilles or AEneas. With historians it is quite the contrary; our thoughts are taken up with the actions, persons, and events we read, and we little regard the authors.

When a true genius appears in the world you may know him by this sign; that the dunces are all in confederacy against him.

Men who possess all the advantages of life, are in a state where there are many accidents to disorder and discompose, but few to please them.

It is unwise to punish cowards with ignominy, for if they had regarded that they would not have been cowards; death is their proper punishment, because they fear it most.

The greatest inventions were produced in the times of ignorance, as the use of the compass, gunpowder, and printing, and by the dullest nation, as the Germans.

One argument to prove that the common relations of ghosts and spectres are generally false, may be drawn from the opinion held that spirits are never seen by more than one person at a time; that is to say, it seldom happens to above one person in a company to be possessed with any high degree of spleen or melancholy.

I am apt to think that, in the day of Judgment, there will be small allowance given to the wise for their want of morals, nor to the ignorant for their want of faith, because both are without excuse. This renders the advantages equal of ignorance and knowledge. But, some scruples in the wise, and some vices in the ignorant, will perhaps be forgiven upon the strength of temptation to each.

The value of several circumstances in story lessens very much by distance of time, though some minute circumstances are very valuable; and it requires great judgment in a writer to distinguish.

It is grown a word of course for writers to say, "This critical age," as divines say, "This sinful age."

It is pleasant to observe how free the present age is in laying taxes on the next. *Future ages shall talk of this; this shall be famous to all posterity*. Whereas their time and thoughts will be taken up about present things, as ours are now.

The chameleon, who is said to feed upon nothing but air, hath, of all animals, the nimblest tongue.

When a man is made a spiritual peer he loses his surname; when a temporal, his Christian name.

It is in disputes as in armies, where the weaker side sets up false lights, and makes a great noise, to make the enemy believe them more numerous and strong than they really are.

Some men, under the notions of weeding out prejudices, eradicate virtue, honesty, and religion.

In all well-instituted commonwealths, care has been taken to limit men's possessions; which is done for many reasons, and among the rest, for one which perhaps is not often considered: that when bounds are set to men's desires, after they have acquired as much as the laws will permit them, their private interest is at an end, and they have nothing to do but to take care of the public.

There are but three ways for a man to revenge himself of the censure of the world: to despise it, to return the like, or to endeavour to live so as to avoid it. The first of these is usually pretended, the last is almost impossible; the universal practice is for the second.

I never heard a finer piece of satire against lawyers than that of astrologers, when they pretend by rules of art to tell when a suit will end, and whether to the advantage of the plaintiff or defendant; thus making the matter depend entirely upon the influence of the stars, without the least regard to the merits of the cause.

The expression in Apocrypha about Tobit and his dog following him I have often heard ridiculed, yet Homer has the same words of Telemachus more than once; and Virgil says something like it of Evander. And I take the book of Tobit to be partly poetical.

I have known some men possessed of good qualities, which were very serviceable to others, but useless to themselves; like a sun-dial on the front of a house, to inform the neighbours and passengers, but not the owner within.

If a man would register all his opinions upon love, politics, religion, learning, etc., beginning from his youth and so go on to old age, what a bundle of inconsistencies and contradictions would appear at last!

What they do in heaven we are ignorant of; what they do not we are told expressly: that they neither marry, nor are given in marriage.

It is a miserable thing to live in suspense; it is the life of a spider.

The Stoical scheme of supplying our wants by lopping off our desires, is like cutting off our feet when we want shoes.

Physicians ought not to give their judgment of religion, for the same reason that butchers are not admitted to be jurors upon life and death.

The reason why so few marriages are happy, is, because young ladies spend their time in making nets, not in making cages.

If a man will observe as he walks the streets, I believe he will find the merriest countenances in mourning coaches.

Nothing more unqualifies a man to act with prudence than a misfortune that is attended with shame and guilt.

The power of fortune is confessed only by the miserable; for the happy impute all their success to prudence or merit.

Ambition often puts men upon doing the meanest offices; so climbing is performed in the same posture with creeping.

Censure is the tax a man pays to the public for being eminent.

Although men are accused for not knowing their own weakness, yet perhaps as few know their own strength. It is, in men as in soils, where sometimes there is a vein of gold which the owner knows not of.

Satire is reckoned the easiest of all wit, but I take it to be otherwise in very bad times: for it is as hard to satirise well a man of distinguished vices, as to praise well a man of distinguished virtues. It is easy enough to do either to people of moderate characters.

Invention is the talent of youth, and judgment of age; so that our judgment grows harder to please, when we have fewer things to offer it: this goes through the whole commerce of life. When we are old, our friends find it difficult to please us, and are less concerned whether we be pleased or no.

No wise man ever wished to be younger.

An idle reason lessens the weight of the good ones you gave before.

The motives of the best actions will not bear too strict an inquiry. It is allowed that the cause of most actions, good or bad, may he resolved into the love of ourselves; but the self-love of some men inclines them to please others, and the self-love of others is wholly employed in pleasing themselves. This makes the great distinction between virtue and vice. Religion is the best motive of all actions, yet religion is allowed to be the highest instance of self-love.

Old men view best at a distance with the eyes of their understanding as well as with those of nature.

Some people take more care to hide their wisdom than their folly.

Anthony Henley's farmer, dying of an asthma, said, "Well, if I can get this breath once *out*, I'll take care it never got *in* again."

The humour of exploding many things under the name of trifles, fopperies, and only imaginary goods, is a very false proof either of wisdom or magnanimity, and a great check to virtuous actions. For instance, with regard to fame, there is in most people a reluctance and unwillingness to be forgotten. We observe, even among the vulgar, how fond they are to have an inscription over their grave. It requires but little philosophy to discover and observe that there is no intrinsic value in all this; however, if it be founded in our nature as an incitement to virtue, it ought not to be ridiculed.

Complaint is the largest tribute heaven receives, and the sincerest part of our devotion.

The common fluency of speech in many men, and most women, is owing to a scarcity of matter, and a scarcity of words; for whoever is a master of language, and hath a mind full of ideas, will be apt, in speaking, to hesitate upon the choice of both; whereas common speakers have only one set of ideas, and one set of words to clothe them in, and these are always ready at the mouth. So people come faster out of a church when it is almost empty, than when a crowd is at the door.

Few are qualified to shine in company; but it is in most men's power to be agreeable. The reason, therefore, why conversation runs so low at present, is not the defect of understanding, but pride, vanity, ill-nature, affectation, singularity, positiveness, or some other vice, the effect of a wrong education.

To be vain is rather a mark of humility than pride. Vain men delight in telling what honours have been done them, what great company they have kept, and the like, by which they plainly confess that these honours were more than their due, and such as their friends would not believe if they had not been told: whereas a man truly proud thinks the greatest honours below his merit, and consequently scorns to boast. I therefore deliver it as a maxim, that whoever desires the character of a proud man, ought to conceal his vanity.

Law, in a free country, is, or ought to be, the determination of the majority of those who have property in land.

One argument used to the disadvantage of Providence I take to be a very strong one in its defence. It is objected that storms and tempests, unfruitful seasons, ser-pents, spiders, flies, and other noxious or troublesome animals, with many more instances of the like kind, discover an imperfection in nature, because human life would be much easier without them; but the design of Providence may clearly be perceived in this proceeding. The motions of the sun and moon--in short, the whole system of the universe, as far as philosophers have been able to discover and observe, are in the utmost degree of regularity and perfection; but wherever God hath left to man the power of interposing a remedy by thought or labour, there he hath placed things in a state of imperfection, on purpose to stir up human industry, without which life would stagnate, or, indeed, rather, could not subsist at all: *Curis accuunt mortalia corda*.

Praise is the daughter of present power.

How inconsistent is man with himself!

I have known several persons of great fame for wisdom in public affairs and counsels governed by foolish servants.

I have known great Ministers, distinguished for wit and learning, who pre-ferred none but dunces.

I have known men of great valour cowards to their wives.

I have known men of the greatest cunning perpetually cheated.

I knew three great Ministers, who could exactly compute and settle the accounts of a kingdom, but were wholly ignorant of their own economy.

The preaching of divines helps to preserve well-inclined men in the course of virtue, but seldom or never reclaims the vicious.

Princes usually make wiser choices than the servants whom they trust for the disposal of places: I have known a prince, more than once, choose an able Minister, but I never observed that Minister to use his credit in the disposal of an employment to a person whom he thought the fittest for it. One of the greatest in this age owned and excused the matter from the violence of parties and the unreasonableness of friends.

Small causes are sufficient to make a man uneasy when great ones are not in the way. For want of a block he will stumble at a straw.

Dignity, high station, or great riches, are in some sort necessary to old men, in order to keep the younger at a distance, who are otherwise too apt to insult them upon the score of their age.

Every man desires to live long; but no man would be old.

Love of flattery in most men proceeds from the mean opinion they have of themselves; in women from the contrary.

If books and laws continue to increase as they have done for fifty years past, I am in some concern for future ages how any man will be learned, or any man a lawyer.

Kings are commonly said to have *long hands*; I wish they had as *long ears*.

Princes in their infancy, childhood, and youth are said to discover prodigious parts and wit, to speak things that surprise and astonish. Strange, so many hopeful princes, and so many shameful kings! If they happen to die young, they would have been prodigies of wisdom and virtue. If they live, they are often prodigies indeed, but of another sort.

Politics, as the word is commonly understood, are nothing but corruptions, and consequently of no use to a good king or a good ministry; for which reason Courts are so overrun with politics.

A nice man is a man of nasty ideas.

Apollo was held the god of physic and sender of diseases. Both were originally the same trade, and still continue.

Old men and comets have been reverenced for the same reason: their long beards, and pretences to foretell events.

A person was asked at court, what he thought of an ambassador and his train, who were all embroidery and lace, full of bows, cringes, and gestures; he said, it was Solomon's importation, gold and apes.

Most sorts of diversion in men, children, and other animals, is an imitation of fighting.

Augustus meeting an ass with a lucky name foretold himself good fortune. I meet many asses, but none of them have lucky names.

If a man makes me keep my distance, the comfort is he keeps his at the same time.

Who can deny that all men are violent lovers of truth when we see them so positive in their errors, which they will maintain out of their zeal to truth, although they contradict themselves every day of their lives?

That was excellently observed, say I, when I read a passage in an author, where his opinion agrees with mine. When we differ, there I pronounce him to be mistaken.

Very few men, properly speaking, live at present, but are providing to live another time.

Laws penned with the utmost care and exactness, and in the vulgar language, are often perverted to wrong meanings; then why should we wonder that the Bible is so?

Although men are accused for not knowing their weakness, yet perhaps as few know their own strength.

A man seeing a wasp creeping into a vial filled with honey, that was hung on a fruit tree, said thus: "Why, thou sottish animal, art thou mad to go into that vial, where you see many hundred of your kind there dying in it before you?" "The reproach is just," answered the wasp, "but not from you men, who are so far from taking example by other people's follies, that you will not take warning by your own. If after falling several times into this vial, and escaping by chance, I should fall in again, I should then but resemble you."

An old miser kept a tame jackdaw, that used to steal pieces of money, and hide them in a hole, which the cat observing, asked why he would hoard up those round shining things that he could make no use of? "Why," said the jackdaw, "my master has a whole chest full, and makes no more use of them than I."

Men are content to be laughed at for their wit, but not for their folly.

If the men of wit and genius would resolve never to complain in their works of critics and detractors, the next age would not know that they ever had any.

After all the maxims and systems of trade and commerce, a stander-by would think the affairs of the world were most ridiculously contrived.

There are few countries which, if well cultivated, would not support double the number of their inhabitants, and yet fewer where one-third of the people are not extremely stinted even in the necessaries of life. I send out twenty barrels of corn, which would maintain a family in bread for a year, and I bring back in return a vessel of wine, which half a dozen good follows would drink in less than a month, at the expense of their health and reason.

A man would have but few spectators, if he offered to show for threepence how he could thrust a red-hot iron into a barrel of gunpowder, and it should not take fire.

NOTES:

{1} Two puppet-show men.
{2} The house-keeper.
{3} The butler.
{4} The footman.
{5} The priest his confessor.

www.bookjungle.com *email: sales@bookjungle.com fax: 630-214-0564 mail: Book Jungle PO Box 2226 Champaign, IL 61825*

### The Codes Of Hammurabi And Moses
### W. W. Davies

QTY

The discovery of the Hammurabi Code is one of the greatest achievements of archaeology, and is of paramount interest, not only to the student of the Bible, but also to all those interested in ancient history...

**Religion**    **ISBN:** *1-59462-338-4*    **Pages:132**
*MSRP $12.95*

### The Theory of Moral Sentiments
### Adam Smith

QTY

This work from 1749. contains original theories of con-science amd moral judgment and it is the foundation for systemof morals.

**Philosophy** **ISBN:** *1-59462-777-0*    **Pages:536**
*MSRP $19.95*

### Jessica's First Prayer
### Hesba Stretton

QTY

In a screened and secluded corner of one of the many railway-bridges which span the streets of London there could be seen a few years ago, from five o'clock every morning until half past eight, a tidily set-out coffee-stall, consisting of a trestle and board, upon which stood two large tin cans, with a small fire of charcoal burning under each so as to keep the coffee boiling during the early hours of the morning when the work-people were thronging into the city on their way to their daily toil...

**Pages:84**

**Childrens**    **ISBN:** *1-59462-373-2*    *MSRP $9.95*

### My Life and Work
### Henry Ford

QTY

Henry Ford revolutionized the world with his implementation of mass production for the Model T automobile. Gain valuable business insight into his life and work with his own auto-biography... "We have only started on our development of our country we have not as yet, with all our talk of wonderful progress, done more than scratch the surface. The progress has been wonderful enough but..."

**Pages:300**

**Biographies/**    **ISBN:** *1-59462-198-5*    *MSRP $21.95*

## The Art of Cross-Examination
## Francis Wellman

QTY

I presume it is the experience of every author, after his first book is published upon an important subject, to be almost overwhelmed with a wealth of ideas and illustrations which could readily have been included in his book, and which to his own mind, at least, seem to make a second edition inevitable. Such certainly was the case with me; and when the first edition had reached its sixth impression in five months, I rejoiced to learn that it seemed to my publishers that the book had met with a sufficiently favorable reception to justify a second and considerably enlarged edition. ..

**Reference**    **ISBN:** *1-59462-647-2*

**Pages:412**

*MSRP $19.95*

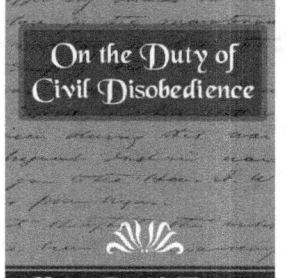

## On the Duty of Civil Disobedience
## Henry David Thoreau

QTY

Thoreau wrote his famous essay, On the Duty of Civil Disobedience, as a protest against an unjust but popular war and the immoral but popular institution of slave-owning. He did more than write—he declined to pay his taxes, and was hauled off to gaol in consequence. Who can say how much this refusal of his hastened the end of the war and of slavery ?

**Law**        **ISBN:** *1-59462-747-9*

**Pages:48**

*MSRP $7.45*

Dream Psychology
Psychoanalysis for Beginners

Sigmund Freud

## Dream Psychology Psychoanalysis for Beginners
## Sigmund Freud

QTY

Sigmund Freud, born Sigismund Schlomo Freud (May 6, 1856 - September 23, 1939), was a Jewish-Austrian neurologist and psychiatrist who co-founded the psychoanalytic school of psychology. Freud is best known for his theories of the unconscious mind, especially involving the mechanism of repression; his redefinition of sexual desire as mobile and directed towards a wide variety of objects; and his therapeutic techniques, especially his understanding of transference in the therapeutic relationship and the presumed value of dreams as sources of insight into unconscious desires.

**Psychology**   **ISBN:** *1-59462-905-6*

**Pages:196**

*MSRP $15.45*

## The Miracle of Right Thought
## Orison Swett Marden

QTY

Believe with all of your heart that you will do what you were made to do. When the mind has once formed the habit of holding cheerful, happy, prosperous pictures, it will not be easy to form the opposite habit. It does not matter how improbable or how far away this realization may see, or how dark the prospects may be, if we visualize them as best we can, as vividly as possible, hold tenaciously to them and vigorously struggle to attain them, they will gradually become actualized, realized in the life. But a desire, a longing without endeavor, a yearning abandoned or held indifferently will vanish without realization.

**Self Help**      **ISBN:** *1-59462-644-8*

**Pages:360**

*MSRP $25.45*

QTY

**The Rosicrucian Cosmo-Conception Mystic Christianity** *by Max Heindel*     ISBN: *1-59462-188-8*   **$38.95**
*The Rosicrucian Cosmo-conception is not dogmatic, neither does it appeal to any other authority than the reason of the student. It is: not controversial, but is: sent forth in the, hope that it may help to clear..*     New Age/Religion Pages 646

**Abandonment To Divine Providence** *by Jean-Pierre de Caussade*     ISBN: *1-59462-228-0*   **$25.95**
*"The Rev. Jean Pierre de Caussade was one of the most remarkable spiritual writers of the Society of Jesus in France in the 18th Century. His death took place at Toulouse in 1751. His works have gone through many editions and have been republished...*     Inspirational/Religion Pages 400

**Mental Chemistry** *by Charles Haanel*     ISBN: *1-59462-192-6*   **$23.95**
*Mental Chemistry allows the change of material conditions by combining and appropriately utilizing the power of the mind. Much like applied chemistry creates something new and unique out of careful combinations of chemicals the mastery of mental chemistry...*     New Age/Business Pages 354

**The Letters of Robert Browning and Elizabeth Barret Barrett 1845-1846 vol II**     ISBN: *1-59462-193-4*   **$35.95**
*by Robert Browning and Elizabeth Barrett*     Biographies Pages 596

**Gleanings In Genesis (volume I)** *by Arthur W. Pink*     ISBN: *1-59462-130-6*   **$27.45**
*Appropriately has Genesis been termed "the seed plot of the Bible" for in it we have, in germ form, almost all of the great doctrines which are afterwards fully developed in the books of Scripture which follow...*     Religion/Inspirational Pages 420

**The Master Key** *by L. W. de Laurence*     ISBN: *1-59462-001-6*   **$30.95**
*In no branch of human knowledge has there been a more lively increase of the spirit of research during the past few years than in the study of Psychology, Concentration and Mental Discipline. The requests for authentic lessons in Thought Control, Mental Discipline and...*     New Age/Business Pages 422

**The Lesser Key Of Solomon Goetia** *by L. W. de Laurence*     ISBN: *1-59462-092-X*   **$9.95**
*This translation of the first book of the "Lernegton" which is now for the first time made accessible to students of Talismanic Magic was done, after careful collation and edition, from numerous Ancient Manuscripts in Hebrew, Latin, and French...*     New Age/Occult Pages 92

**Rubaiyat Of Omar Khayyam** *by Edward Fitzgerald*     ISBN:*1-59462-332-5*   **$13.95**
*Edward Fitzgerald, whom the world has already learned, in spite of his own efforts to remain within the shadow of anonymity, to look upon as one of the rarest poets of the century, was born at Bredfield, in Suffolk, on the 31st of March, 1809. He was the third son of John Purcell...*     Music Pages 172

**Ancient Law** *by Henry Maine*     ISBN: *1-59462-128-4*   **$29.95**
*The chief object of the following pages is to indicate some of the earliest ideas of mankind, as they are reflected in Ancient Law, and to point out the relation of those ideas to modern thought.*     Religiom/History Pages 452

**Far-Away Stories** *by William J. Locke*     ISBN: *1-59462-129-2*   **$19.45**
*"Good wine needs no bush, but a collection of mixed vintages does. And this book is just such a collection. Some of the stories I do not want to remain buried for ever in the museum files of dead magazine-numbers an author's not unpardonable vanity..."*     Fiction Pages 272

**Life of David Crockett** *by David Crockett*     ISBN: *1-59462-250-7*   **$27.45**
*"Colonel David Crockett was one of the most remarkable men of the times in which he lived. Born in humble life, but gifted with a strong will, an indomitable courage, and unremitting perseverance...*     Biographies/New Age Pages 424

**Lip-Reading** *by Edward Nitchie*     ISBN: *1-59462-206-X*   **$25.95**
*Edward B. Nitchie, founder of the New York School for the Hard of Hearing, now the Nitchie School of Lip-Reading, Inc, wrote "LIP-READING Principles and Practice". The development and perfecting of this meritorious work on lip-reading was an undertaking...*     How-to Pages 400

**A Handbook of Suggestive Therapeutics, Applied Hypnotism, Psychic Science**     ISBN: *1-59462-214-0*   **$24.95**
*by Henry Munro*     Health/New Age/Health/Self-help Pages 376

**A Doll's House: and Two Other Plays** *by Henrik Ibsen*     ISBN: *1-59462-112-8*   **$19.95**
*Henrik Ibsen created this classic when in revolutionary 1848 Rome. Introducing some striking concepts in playwriting for the realist genre, this play has been studied the world over.*     Fiction/Classics/Plays 308

**The Light of Asia** *by sir Edwin Arnold*     ISBN: *1-59462-204-3*   **$13.95**
*In this poetic masterpiece, Edwin Arnold describes the life and teachings of Buddha. The man who was to become known as Buddha to the world was born as Prince Gautama of India but he rejected the worldly riches and abandoned the reigns of power when...*     Religion/History/Biographies Pages 170

**The Complete Works of Guy de Maupassant** *by Guy de Maupassant*     ISBN: *1-59462-157-8*   **$16.95**
*"For days and days, nights and nights, I had dreamed of that first kiss which was to consecrate our engagement, and I knew not on what spot I should put my lips..."*     Fiction/Classics Pages 240

**The Art of Cross-Examination** *by Francis L. Wellman*     ISBN: *1-59462-309-0*   **$26.95**
*Written by a renowned trial lawyer, Wellman imparts his experience and uses case studies to explain how to use psychology to extract desired information through questioning.*     How-to/Science/Reference Pages 408

**Answered or Unanswered?** *by Louisa Vaughan*     ISBN: *1-59462-248-5*   **$10.95**
*Miracles of Faith in China*     Religion Pages 112

**The Edinburgh Lectures on Mental Science (1909)** *by Thomas*     ISBN: *1-59462-008-3*   **$11.95**
*This book contains the substance of a course of lectures recently given by the writer in the Queen Street Hail, Edinburgh. Its purpose is to indicate the Natural Principles governing the relation between Mental Action and Material Conditions...*     New Age/Psychology Pages 148

**Ayesha** *by H. Rider Haggard*     ISBN: *1-59462-301-5*   **$24.95**
*Verily and indeed it is the unexpected that happens! Probably if there was one person upon the earth from whom the Editor of this, and of a certain previ-ous history, did not expect to hear again...*     Classics Pages 380

**Ayala's Angel** *by Anthony Trollope*     ISBN: *1-59462-352-X*   **$29.95**
*The two girls were both pretty, but Lucy who was twenty-one who supposed to be simple and comparatively unattractive, whereas Ayala was credited, as her Bombwhat romantic name might show, with poetic charm and a taste for romance. Ayala when her father died was nineteen...*     Fiction Pages 484

**The American Commonwealth** *by James Bryce*     ISBN: *1-59462-286-8*   **$34.45**
*An interpretation of American democratic political theory. It examines political mechanics and society from the perspective of Scotsman James Bryce*     Politics Pages 572

**Stories of the Pilgrims** *by Margaret P. Pumphrey*     ISBN: *1-59462-116-0*   **$17.95**
*This book explores pilgrims religious oppression in England as well as their escape to Holland and eventual crossing to America on the Mayflower, and their early days in New England...*     History Pages 268

QTY

**The Fasting Cure** *by Sinclair Upton*                                    ISBN: *1-59462-222-1*    **$13.95**
*In the Cosmopolitan Magazine for May, 1910, and in the Contemporary Review (London) for April, 1910, I published an article dealing with my experiences in fasting. I have written a great many magazine articles, but never one which attracted so much attention... New Age/Self Help/Health Pages 164*

**Hebrew Astrology** *by Sepharial*                                    ISBN: *1-59462-308-2*    **$13.45**
*In these days of advanced thinking it is a matter of common observation that we have left many of the old landmarks behind and that we are now pressing forward to greater heights and to a wider horizon than that which represented the mind-content of our progenitors...    Astrology Pages 144*

**Thought Vibration or The Law of Attraction in the Thought World**    ISBN: *1-59462-127-6*    **$12.95**
*by William Walker Atkinson*                                        *Psychology/Religion Pages 144*

**Optimism** *by Helen Keller*                                        ISBN: *1-59462-108-X*    **$15.95**
*Helen Keller was blind, deaf, and mute since 19 months old, yet famously learned how to overcome these handicaps, communicate with the world, and spread her lectures promoting optimism. An inspiring read for everyone...    Biographies/Inspirational Pages 84*

**Sara Crewe** *by Frances Burnett*                                    ISBN: *1-59462-360-0*    **$9.45**
*In the first place, Miss Minchin lived in London. Her home was a large, dull, tall one, in a large, dull square, where all the houses were alike, and all the sparrows were alike, and where all the door-knockers made the same heavy sound...    Childrens/Classic Pages 88*

**The Autobiography of Benjamin Franklin** *by Benjamin Franklin*    ISBN: *1-59462-135-7*    **$24.95**
*The Autobiography of Benjamin Franklin has probably been more extensively read than any other American historical work, and no other book of its kind has had such ups and downs of fortune. Franklin lived for many years in England, where he was agent...    Biographies/History Pages 332*

| Name | |
| --- | --- |
| Email | |
| Telephone | |
| Address | |
| | |
| City, State ZIP | |

☐ Credit Card          ☐ Check / Money Order

| Credit Card Number | |
| --- | --- |
| Expiration Date | |
| Signature | |

*Please Mail to:   Book Jungle*
*PO Box 2226*
*Champaign, IL 61825*
*or Fax to:        630-214-0564*

## ORDERING INFORMATION

**web***: www.bookjungle.com*
**email***: sales@bookjungle.com*
**fax***: 630-214-0564*
**mail***: Book Jungle  PO Box 2226  Champaign, IL 61825*
**or PayPal** *to sales@bookjungle.com*

*Please contact us for bulk discounts*

## DIRECT-ORDER TERMS

**20% Discount if You Order
Two or More Books**
Free Domestic Shipping!
Accepted: Master Card, Visa,
Discover, American Express